"It's high time someone stood up to you!"

Anger and defiance flashed from Jessica's eyes as she waited to hear how Luke would respond to her challenge.

"Really?" he said. "Is that what you think?" To her surprise he smiled. It was devastating.

She blinked and tried to move away. "That's what I think," she spat out.

Abruptly, in one deft movement, he pulled her close, so that her body was pressed against the lean, hard length of his. "And tell me, Jessica, what do you think of this?" His arm slid around her back, pinning her to his chest, and before she could turn her head, his mouth claimed hers, fiercely, compellingly.

And suddenly, Jessica could not think at all....

STEPHANIE HOWARD is a British author whose two ambitions since childhood were to see the world and write. Her first venture into the world was a four-year stay in Italy, learning the language and supporting herself by writing short stories. Then her sensible side brought her back to London to read Social Administrations at the London School of Economics. She has held various editorial posts at magazines such as *Reader's Digest*, *Vanity Fair*, *Women's Own*, as well as writing freelance for *Cosmopolitan*, *Good Housekeeping* and *The Observer*. However, she has spent the past six years happily trotting around the globe before returning to the U.K. to write.

Books by Stephanie Howard

HARLEQUIN PRESENTS
1098—RELUCTANT PRISONER

Don't miss any of our special offers. Write to us at the following address for information on our newest releases.

Harlequin Reader Service
901 Fuhrmann Blvd., P.O. Box 1397, Buffalo, NY 14240
Canadian address: P.O. Box 603,
Fort Erie, Ont. L2A 5X3

STEPHANIE HOWARD

HOWARD

dark lucifer

Harlequin Books

TORONTO • NEW YORK • LONDON
AMSTERDAM • PARIS • SYDNEY • HAMBURG
STOCKHOLM • ATHENS • TOKYO • MILAN

Harlequin Presents first edition December 1988
ISBN 0-373-11130-4

Original hardcover edition published in 1988
by Mills & Boon Limited

CHAPTER ONE

JESSICA didn't notice the sleek black Porsche that was following her as she turned into the auction rooms' car park, and manoeuvred the old, white-painted van into a convenient space near the rear entrance door.

Nor was she aware of how the driver hung back at a safe distance to watch her as she climbed out, allowing a brief flicker of pride to illuminate her dark green eyes as she glanced at the legend on the side of the van. Bridge Antiques. Even now, almost three years since she had first taken over the business, she still felt a thrill of satisfaction at the sight of it. Whoever would have thought the once penniless Jessica Langley would one day be running her own antiques business?

High heels clicking confidently, her shoulder-length chestnut hair swinging as she went, she strode obliviously across the tarmac to the saleroom door. A tall, striking figure in a slim blue suit. Classy and elegant, yet with an underlying promise of sensuality—as the driver of the Porsche could not help but appreciate as he watched, waiting till she had disappeared inside before parking his vehicle almost directly opposite the old white van. What a pity fate had cast him as her enemy!

If Jessica failed to notice the stranger, it was because she had other, more pressing, matters on her mind. This afternoon's sale that she had just driven twenty-five miles into Tunbridge Wells to attend was important. Very important—for the future of Bridge Antiques and for her own personal happiness as well. Not that she was unduly concerned. Matters both professional and private, she believed, were firmly set on an upward path.

'Good afternoon, Miss Langley. Glad you could make it.' A moustached, military-looking gentleman, whom Jessica recognized as one of the local organisers of the sale, greeted her with a friendly smile as she made her way into the steadily filling hall. 'I think we've got quite a number of things to interest you this afternoon.'

'You certainly have, colonel,' she smiled back at him. 'I expect to go home tonight with a full vanload.'

The colonel nodded approvingly at her. 'Your aunt would be proud if she could see what you've made of the business,' he said. 'What you've accomplished is nothing short of a miracle. I know you won't mind me saying that very few people ever thought you'd make a go of it.'

Jessica laughed. How could she mind? When old Aunt Polly had died three years ago and left her run-down antiques shop in rural Kent, along with the tiny flat above that went with it, Jessica had been an inexperienced girl of twenty who knew nothing about running a business of any kind—and even less about antiques. Hard work, long hours of study and an almost pathological inability to quit were what had worked the so-called miracle.

'I had to make a go of it,' she told the colonel with a light-hearted wink. 'We Langleys don't like to be beaten, you know.' Besides, she reminded herself privately, she'd had absolutely nothing to lose. Alone in the world after the recent deaths of her parents, and working in London at a dead-end job she loathed, she'd seen the challenge of her unexpected inheritance as a God-sent opportunity. Without a qualm, she'd upped stakes and moved south to Harbingdon, rolled up her sleeves and set about building a worthwhile future for herself.

And she had succeeded almost beyond her wildest dreams. Why, just a matter of weeks ago, some anonymous individual had offered to buy her out for a sum she could only have dreamed of three years ago.

The colonel gave her an admiring nod. 'It's nice to see someone doing so well in these difficult days.' Then he paused, 'And Mr Cole? Is he well?'

Jessica smiled at the mention of her fiancé. 'Very well, thank you. He's off to a sale up in Northampton today. We're trying to build up our stock for the summer season now.' A move which was absolutely vital if they were to attract the all-important tourist trade. Vital, too, for the long-term prospects of Bridge Antiques. For this could be the season they finally turned the corner and really established themselves. Then she and Graham could at last become partners in marriage, as well as partners in business.

'Well, keep up the good work, my dear.' The colonel patted her arm affectionately as he took his leave. 'And I hope you manage to get everything you're after today.'

Unaware of the eyes that followed her now, Jessica took a seat near the front and glanced round with interest at the packed hall. There were several faces that she recognised—mostly dealers like herself, either local or from London or further afield—and she smiled and exchanged greetings with several of them. It pleased her to know that she was both liked and respected among the other members of her trade. It had cost her a sacrifice in blood, sweat and tears to carve out her little professional niche, but every ounce of agony had been worthwhile.

A crackle of anticipation went round the room as, at last, the auctioneer appeared and made preparations to begin. And, as always on such occasions, Jessica felt the sharp thrust of excitement as the adrenalin began to flow. She literally revelled in the knife-edge atmosphere of the auction room. The cut and thrust of the bidding, like sword-play. The spills, the falls, the surprises. And the magic elation when one managed to secure one's prize.

Anxious to get started now, she slipped from her bag the sheaf of papers with the careful notes she'd made at the preliminary viewing earlier in the week. Listed was every item that had caught her eye, along with precise calculations of the very top bid she could afford to make for each of them. And she leaned forward expectantly as Lot One was announced.

The first dozen or so items to come under the hammer were not on her list, but she followed the bidding with close attention none the less, hoping to gauge the prevailing atmosphere. And it seemed good. The prices being commanded so far were fair to average. With a bit of luck, she might manage to walk off with a bargain or two.

Then her ears pricked up as the auctioneer announced the first item on her list, a little mahogany side table, and started the bidding at a cautious two hundred pounds. In a discreet signal, Jessica raised the sheaf of papers in her hand.

'Two hundred and fifty,' the auctioneer announced.

Then, on a nod from the bald-pated gentleman seated two rows in front of her, a dealer from the Midlands she'd often had to bid against before, the price rose to three hundred pounds.

Again Jessica signalled that she was still in the race. But her bald-headed adversary was still in it, too.

'Four hundred,' the auctioneer called and glanced round at the assembled gathering.

Jessica made her final bid. Four hundred and fifty pounds was as high as she could afford to go. The bald head in front shook resignedly and Jessica smiled triumphantly to herself.

'Ladies and gentlemen, do I have your final bid?' The hammer was poised. It looked like her first acquisition of the day was already safely in the bag. Her eyes dropped confidently to the catalogue to check on what was coming up next.

'I am bid five hundred pounds!'

With a start of disbelief, Jessica's eyes jerked up to the auctioneer again. Where had that last bid come from? And she felt a hot stab of irritation as she acknowledged that her budget would not let her better it. She watched in dumb annoyance as the hammer cracked down once, twice, three times, and the auctioneer announced in his impassive voice, 'Sold to the gentleman in the middle of the room.'

She resisted the urge to turn around. Damn him, whoever he was! It was not a good start, but there was plenty more for her to bid for yet. But on the next two she tried for, a set of dining chairs and a carved oak desk, exactly the same thing happened again. She was outbid just at the moment when she thought the prize was hers.

'Sold to the gentleman in the middle of the room.'

Impatiently, Jessica pursed her lips and continued to stare furiously straight ahead. Who the devil was this "gentleman in the middle of the room" who seemed so hellbent on outbidding her? Twice could pass as a coincidence. Three times was beginning to look distinctly like a pattern. But there was no way he would wrest the next piece from her, she resolved. She already had a certain buyer for the roll-top desk. She'd go over her budget and pare down her profit margin to a minimum, if necessary, but this one was very definitely hers!

The bidding started and moved ahead quickly, with offers coming from all corners of the room. It was a particularly pretty piece and she'd expected to have to put up a fight. Originally, she'd decided that six hundred and fifty pounds was as high as she would go, but she mentally upped that now to eight hundred. Her client was a good and regular customer. It would be bad business for her to let him down.

'I am bid seven hundred pounds.' The auctioneer cast a searching eye around his audience as the bidders rapidly began to thin out.

With an aggressive tightening of her jaw, Jessica quickly raised her hand.

'Seven hundred and fifty, I am bid.'

But it was not enough. The auctioneer's eyes moved to the middle of the room. 'Eight hundred.'

Jessica clenched her fists—him again!—and signalled once more. 'Eight hundred and fifty.'

She'd gone even higher than her revised upper limit now, and wiped out any profit worth mentioning. But she didn't care. The desk was hers. Only a madman would take the bidding any higher.

'Nine hundred pounds!'

Jessica gasped in mingled outrage and disbelief and swung round, green eyes flashing, unable to suppress her anger and curiosity any more. Who was this insufferable individual who seemed intent on ruining her afternoon? What sort of game was he playing, anyway?

It was no game. Something inside her went curiously cold as she found herself staring into his face. A face of hard, dark lines, commanding, almost demonic in the savage strength that it portrayed. And the eyes, black and forbidding as they stared with an unnerving stark ferocity back into hers.

'Sold to the gentleman in the middle of the room!'

As the auctioneer's hammer came down, the fine, straight lips curved in a mirthless smile and abruptly Jessica turned away, chilled by the undisguised hostility in him. Who was he? she asked herself again. And why had he looked at her as though he hated her?

As the sale went on, she struggled to dismiss him from her mind. But it was impossible. For one thing, he continued to outbid her on every single item she went after—the only items, it had grown clear, that he showed any interest in at all. And for another, she was uncomfortably aware of those piercing dark eyes boring into her back. Whoever he was, he was out to thwart her, and it seemed there wasn't a single thing that she could do.

'But don't think you're going to get away with it!' Jessica muttered angrily to herself. 'I can play dirty, too, when I'm pushed far enough!'

One of the pieces near the bottom of her list was a fine English mahogany *secrétaire* that she knew could sell without any difficulty at all. But what hope did she have of securing it with this madman around? Zero. She sat back in her seat with sudden resolve and folded her arms across her chest. So, let him have it, since he was determined to snatch everything else from her. And she smiled with secret pleasure to herself. But let him have it at a price. He'd outbid her on every single piece she'd wanted—let him do the same with this. Only this time she'd take him to the limit first. His nasty little game was about to backfire in his face!

The auctioneer started the bidding and Jessica could feel the bloodlust in her start to rise as her own third bid was topped, taking the price to a giddy sixteen hundred pounds. But this was only the start of the contest. The price was spiralling up past the two thousand mark.

'Two thousand, four hundred pounds!'

Jessica took a deep breath. Now the only bidders left were herself and a dealer sitting at the front. But she knew that her dark adversary was simply waiting till she was on her own. Only then would he join in. Resolutely, she raised her hand. This was no game for the faint-hearted. If she was to have her revenge, then she must keep her nerve.

The auctioneer acknowledged her latest bid. 'Two thousand, five hundred pounds.' Then there was a pause as the dealer in the front row signalled that he was dropping out. Finally, she was on her own! Then the sharp eyes of the auctioneer moved to the middle of the room. 'Two thousand, six hundred,' he announced.

Jessica clenched her fists in self-congratulation and delight. So he'd fallen for it! Now she would teach him the lesson he deserved. Warming to her mission of revenge, once more she raised her hand.

'Two thousand, seven hundred pounds.'

And instantly he bettered it.

It was all that Jessica could do now to contain her glee. Again she signalled to the auctioneer. And again the dark stranger was in with a higher bid.

An almost funereal hush had fallen across the hall as all attention focused now on the two central gladiators locked in their private duel. And the atmosphere, already tense, almost exploded as Jessica took the bidding to three thousand, one hundred pounds. The real value of the *secrétaire* had ceased to matter long ago. This was a battle of wills. No more, no less.

Dry-mouthed, Jessica waited for him to better her bid—which he did, almost instantaneously—and she hugged herself inwardly with anticipation as the clench of excitement in the pit of her stomach tightened almost unbearably. She would take him to four thousand pounds, she decided, then drop out. Let there be a little mercy in the world.

And it was so easy. She hardly had to raise her hand at all before he jumped in with a higher bid. The man was obsessed. It was all she could do to resist turning round to survey him with a gloating smile.

'Three thousand, six hundred pounds.'

Jessica signalled three thousand and seven. Her heart was fluttering like a demented bird. Her nerves stretched like piano wire. But release was almost at hand as, automatically, he upped her bid. Then, for the last time, she signalled and sat back with a wicked smile to enjoy the glorious climax of her little game.

But it did not come. She saw the eyes of the auctioneer move expectantly to the middle of the room. Then, ominously, back to her again. He cleared his throat. 'I have three thousand, nine hundred pounds. Ladies and gentlemen, is this your final bid?'

For one ghastly moment, Jessica could not believe her ears. What was the damned man waiting for? Then her heart lurched sickeningly inside her breast as the auctioneer's hammer started to come down.

'Once . . . Twice . . .'

Quivering with anger, she spun round in her seat, aware that her cheeks had turned deathly pale. The steely eyes in the strong, bronzed face met hers with a glint of ruthless triumph in their depths, and again the lips curled in a mirthless smile.

'Bastard!' she hissed at him beneath her breath, as the auctioneer's hammer descended for the third and final time.

'Sold to Miss Langley for three thousand, nine hundred pounds!'

Choking with rage, she swung away and stumbled blindly to her feet. There was no point in staying on any longer now. For one thing, she had no more money left to spend. She'd just blown her entire budget for the day. For another, she feared she might suffer a coronary if she stayed in the same room for another second with this man.

Of course, it was partly her own fault, she acknowledged bitterly as she led the porters out to the car park to load the ill-starred bureau into her van. She had made the unforgivable error of underestimating her adversary, had momentarily dropped her guard and allowed him to do to her precisely what she'd planned to do to him. And it had cost her dearly. She was lumbered with a white elephant that, if she were lucky, would realize half of what she'd paid for it. Her mysterious opponent had proved to be a great deal cleverer than she'd initially given him credit for.

It was just as she was slamming shut the rear door of the van that she noticed the black Porsche parked, somewhat ominously, opposite.

'Some set of wheels,' remarked one of the porters, following her gaze with open admiration in his eyes.

'Indeed.' But it wasn't admiration that Jessica felt. A blinding anger and resentment more like. For she knew in a flash who the owner of the car must be. Its powerful, dark, aggressive lines were somehow in total keeping with the man. Quickly, she tipped the porters and climbed behind the wheel of the van. The sooner she got out of here and as far away as possible, the happier she would start to feel.

The engine of the old van turned over reluctantly. 'Come on,' she coaxed. 'Don't you start

playing up as well!' And she breathed a sigh of relief
as it finally caught. The very last thing she could
have tolerated now was to be stranded here with the
risk that that infernal man might suddenly appear.
And she jammed the engine into gear and headed
impatiently for the highway just as the first drops
of rain began to fall.

A mile up the road, the heavens opened. 'That's
all I need!' she grumbled irritably to herself. And
she clutched at the steering wheel and fought to
keep her concentration on the road. But her brain
was a-whirr with distracting images of the man who
had just robbed her of a potentially profitable
afternoon—and hoodwinked her into virtually
throwing away four thousand pounds that she could
ill afford. And that was why, just about five miles
outside Harbingdon, she made her next fatal
mistake. She took a corner far too fast, swerved,
skidded on the slippery road and swore as a spray
of stones strafed her windscreen, shattering it.

Blindly, she jammed on the brakes and came to
an ungainly, slewing halt on the wrong side of the
road. 'Now you've done it!' she admonished
herself. 'What an idiotic thing to do!' And she
angrily punched out the shattered windscreen with
her fist. Now she would have to drive the rest of
the way with this downpour lashing in her face!

Barely controlling her temper now, she twisted
the starter key with a trembling hand. The engine
coughed, whimpered pathetically, then died. She
tried again—nothing. And again—still nothing. She
thumped the steering wheel with all her strength.
'Start, damn you!' It was beginning to feel as
though somebody had put a jinx on her.

It was a quiet road, miles from a telephone. Her only hope was that some passing motorist would come to her aid. She climbed out and yanked open the bonnet, a fairly universal signal of distress. Then she stood there, peering impatiently up and down the narrow country road as the wind tugged at the thin jacket and skirt she wore and the rain plastered her hair in dripping tendrils to her face and neck. She shivered. At this rate, she could end up in bed for a week on top of everything else. If no one passed within the next quarter of an hour or so, she'd have to start thinking about walking home.

But then, just as she was about to despair, a dark speck appeared beyond the furthest bend of the wood-lined road, heading towards her rapidly. Relief swept through her as she jumped out into the middle of the road and frantically began to wave her arms. She was saved! But her relief turned to horror as the car drew close enough for her to recognise.

'Oh, no!' She sprang back, dropping her arms, and prayed that it would drive on by.

But today was not a good day for prayers, as Jessica should have known by now. A moment later, the sleek black Porsche purred to a halt, inches away from her, and the electronically operated driver's window slid down soundlessly.

'Trouble?' He spoke the query more with satisfaction than with sympathy.

She scowled at him. From the short distance that separated them now, she could see that he was somewhere in his early thirties, that his eyes were dark grey, flecked with gold and that his hair looked almost black against the collar of his fine white shirt. The suntanned face was strongly boned, even more commanding close to than it had been from afar, and the fine, mobile mouth was wide and passionate-looking. It was a good face, a memorable face. The face of a man to be reckoned with.

But all of this she registered quite unconsciously. There was nothing of approval, only cool contempt in her eyes now, as she answered, 'It won't start, if that's what you mean.'

He looked past her, unperturbed. 'Your windscreen's gone.'

She pushed the wet hair from her face, hating him for his composure, and herself even more for her untimely lack of it. 'I'm perfectly aware of that,' she snapped, squinting quickly up and down the road, hoping to see another car. But there was none.

'Not much traffic on these little country lanes, is there? You could be stuck here for quite a while.' He studied her face for a moment, and she could tell that he was loving every humiliating second of this. 'It hasn't exactly been your day, Miss Langley, has it, now?'

She glared at him. 'It was going all right until *you* came along! Why don't you just get on your way and leave me alone?'

He shook his head. 'Dear, dear. That would be most unchivalrous. I'm afraid I can't offer to fix your van for you, but I can give you a bit of free advice. Whatever's wrong with it, I doubt you're doing things much good by leaving the bonnet open like that.'

The same thought had occurred to her. With an angry flourish, she turned and slammed the bonnet shut.

'And now I'd advise you to climb in here and allow me to drive you home. Fortunately, it's on my way.'

She would sooner have climbed into a dark hole with a tarantula. 'No, thanks!' she spat at him. 'I'd rather walk!' And she was just about to turn her back on him when a treacherous gust of wind caught at the front of her jacket, flinging the flimsy lapels aside to expose the rain-drenched cotton blouse she wore beneath, totally transparent now, as it clung provocatively to her bra-less breasts. As his eyes travelled appreciatively downwards, she hastily snatched her jacket shut again. 'Haven't you already had enough entertainment at my expense? Go and bother someone else!'

Amusement flickered momentarily in the gold-flecked eyes. 'Don't be a damned fool. You could wait here for hours for someone else to pass. And you can't possibly walk in this deluge. It's more than five miles to Harbingdon.'

She peered at him through narrowed, suspicious eyes. 'How do you know where I live, anyway?'

He laughed, a cynical, almost bitter-sounding laugh. 'I know a great deal about you, Jessica Langley. A very great deal indeed.' Then he gestured impatiently and slid the window half-closed. 'Now get in if you're coming. I don't enjoy getting soaked, even if you do.'

Jessica stared down at her sodden feet, the blue of her suit, drenched now almost to black. What choice did she really have? He was right, she could wait for ever for another car to pass. And five miles in this downpour was quite a hike. What was the point of piling even more agony on herself? Besides, a lift was really the very least he owed her, after all. And, if she was perfectly honest with herself, her curiosity was stirred.

She made up her mind. 'OK'—as he very pointedly began to rev the Porche's engine up. 'I'll get my bag.'

She turned and sprinted to the van, grabbing her bag from where she had left it on the driver's seat. And when she got back to the Porsche, the passenger door was standing open for her.

'I hope you've locked the van up well.' He threw her a mocking sideways glance as she climbed in, clutching her tan leather bag protectively to her sodden chest. 'We wouldn't want anyone stealing that precious *secrétaire* of yours.'

So he was adding insult now to injury. As the car moved off silently, she turned to fix him with a steely stare. 'I suppose that's how you get your kicks,' she accused, tight-lipped. 'Tricking innocent tradespeople into spending money they can't afford.'

The dark eyes raked her face with a scathing look. 'Don't try to play the innocent with me. You were the one who was trying to play tricks.' He turned his attention back to the road. 'And that was neither a sensible nor a profitable thing to do.'

Yes. Hadn't she learned that to her cost? Jessica said nothing, but sat back in her seat and glanced ruefully across at him through lowered lids.

He was dressed in a dark, immaculately tailored suit. Broad-shouldered. Tall, she guessed. And the fingers that gripped the steering wheel were long and square-tipped, sensitive like a surgeon's hands. His arms would be strongly muscled, deeply tanned, and she could sense the whiplash power that lay beneath the fine, taut fabric that encased his thighs. His shoes, she observed, were of fine black lizardskin, and it struck her that his shirts and underwear were more than likely monogrammed. Instantly rebuking herself for such an outrageous thought, she automatically inched away from him.

'What's the matter? Are you afraid of me?'

'Not in the slightest.' But it was not quite true.

'Perhaps you ought to be.' An unmistakable note of menace sounded in his voice.

'Why?' Jessica felt an uneasy fluttering in the pit of her stomach at his words. 'Who are you, anyway?'

'Who am I?' He turned and smiled a tiger's predatory smile. Then paused, before adding in a warning voice, 'Someone, I promise, you'll be sorry that you ever met.'

She forced a wan smile. 'Is that your idea of a joke?'

'No joke, I assure you.' He turned to fix her with a pair of eyes as cold as pebbles in a mountain stream. 'This afternoon, you see, was just the start.'

Jessica's fingers tightened around her bag, sudden indignation welling in her now. 'Are you trying to threaten me?'

'Not threaten. I merely wish to advise you of my intent.'

'Is that what you call it? Advising me of your intent? Well, that's quite a euphemism, isn't it?' She was trembling with anger and outrage now.

How dared this stranger come into her life and start trampling all over everything she'd had to struggle so hard for? Her green eyes flashed accusingly at him. 'I can see you're obviously a wealthy man. Perhaps it amuses you to play pathetic little power games with someone like me, who's in no position to stand up to you. Throwing away a few thousand pounds in an afternoon for the dubious pleasure of seeing your defenceless victim squirm is probably your idea of a bit of sport. Well, it isn't mine. I work damned hard to make a living, and I don't appreciate someone like you coming along and trying to screw it up simply for the hell of it!'

She sat back, still shaking with fury, but her little tirade had left him quite unmoved. 'Nice speech, Miss Langley,' he observed. 'But I'm afraid you're not much of a judge of character. I don't do things like this just for the hell of it. And it's not a game. Believe me, I'm deadly serious.'

She dropped her eyes, feeling again the chill she had felt when she had first realized that he was serious, back in the auction room. 'Then, why? Why are you doing this to me?'

He threw her an unsympathetic smile. 'Don't play the victim, Miss Langley, please. You had your chance to avoid all this unpleasantness, and you turned it down.'

She frowned at him, genuinely baffled. 'What do you mean?'

'Were you not offered the chance, just over a month ago, to sell up and get out while the going was good?'

Jessica blinked. He could only be referring to the offer she'd received from an unknown source for her fifty per cent of the business. And since she'd told no one about it—not even her fiancé and brand-new business partner, Graham—how could this stranger possibly know? Unless he'd been behind it, of course. Her eyes narrowed. 'So it was you?'

He flicked her a critical glance. 'It was most unwise of you to turn me down.'

Financially, perhaps. The offer, received anonymously through her solicitor, had mentioned a settlement figure close to what the business as a whole was worth. With that sort of recompense, she could easily have washed her hands of Bridge Antiques and started up again elsewhere. Which was exactly what the letter accompanying the offer had suggested that she do. But it had never crossed her mind for a single moment to accept. Bridge Antiques meant far too much to her for that. 'I've no intention of selling,' she told him now.

'Then you must accept the consequences.' Again the edge of menace sounded in his voice. 'I warned you in my letter it would be financial suicide to hang on. And I can assure you I was not exaggerating.'

Jessica straightened defiantly in her seat. 'You also made some filthy, if ludicrous, allegations against my fiancé,' she accused, suddenly remembering the details with the same distaste she had experienced on first reading them.

'There was nothing ludicrous about those allegations,' he assured her now. 'Cole is a cheat and a swindler—as I gave you every opportunity to check out for yourself. The names and addresses of at least a dozen of the people whose lives he has destroyed were listed in that letter. Did you take the trouble to follow any of them up?'

'Certainly not!' She glared indignantly at him. The very idea was preposterous!

'Then I suggest you do.' The fine mouth twisted contemptuously as he spoke. 'Unless, of course, you already know all about your partner's nefarious activities—and condone them. I realise that also is a possibility.' Then, when she turned angrily away from him, disdaining to defend herself, he added coldly, 'That, of course, is your affair. It simply means I am compelled to destroy you as well in the process of bringing Cole to his knees.'

A shiver ran through her, due only in small part to the dampness of her clothes, as she glanced across at the dark, implacable profile, half wishing now that she'd refused his offer of a lift and walked. The very worst she would have risked then was a dose of flu. This man, she sensed, was capable of bringing something much worse down upon her head. With an effort, she kept her tone steady as she demanded, 'Even if all those accusations in that letter were true—which I know beyond the slightest doubt that they are not—what has it to do with you? Are you some kind of avenging angel or something?'

He smiled then, revealing teeth that were strong and even, very white. 'An angel of any description is something I have never professed to be.'

No, she thought bleakly. The devil incarnate would be closer to the truth.

He went on, 'As much as I despise what Cole did to those people, they are not the reason I intend to make his life a misery. My reason is much more personal than that.' The grey eyes flicked round briefly then to scan her face. 'The purpose of making that information available to you was quite simply to demonstrate what manner of individual you've got yourself entangled with. To make it that much easier for you to extricate yourself. And I'm prepared to give you one last chance. Sell me your share of the business, wash your hands of that rogue, Cole—and I guarantee that you can walk away unscathed.'

'Never!' Jessica forced herself to meet the dark gaze unflinchingly, though there was real fear fluttering in her heart. 'I don't know what you're really up to or why you decided to pick on me, but you're wrong if you think you can either bribe or bully me into handing over Bridge Antiques. I'll fight you if I have to. Every single step of the way!'

'Then you'll be wasting your time and your energy,' he promised with a sadistic smile. 'For there's no way you can win. I'll break you—both of you. That I can absolutely guarantee.'

Hastily, Jessica dropped her eyes. He had spoken the words at her like a curse, sending an icy draught like winter shivering to her very soul. She sat back stiffly in her seat as they drove the rest of the way in silence, the only sounds the incessant drumming of the rain and the whirr of the single windscreen wiper as it beat the constant stream aside. Who was he? she wondered, not daring to meet that dark, mesmeric gaze again. Some madman? No, he was not that. Some demon, then, in the guise of a man, come to lay his evil spell on her? And she pulled the damp jacket closer around her shoulders and peered out into the gathering gloom. Let them get to Harbingdon soon!

It was as they were sweeping through the village and up the hill towards the shop that he broke the silence. 'It's very pretty here,' he remarked in a deceptively conversational tone of voice. Then, as she turned to nod agreement with the sentiment, he added with a callous smile, 'Enjoy it while you can, my dear. You may not have much longer here.'

Abruptly, the car stopped and, trembling, Jessica grappled with the door-handle, almost falling to the rain-washed pavement in her hurry to escape. A welter of emotions raged through her: anger, outrage, indignation, fear. As she made to slam the car door shut, he leaned across and caught it deftly with his hand.

'Goodbye, Jessica Langley,' he intoned with a demonic smile. 'I'll give you twenty-four hours to change your mind.' And he thrust a small, embossed business card into her hand. 'You can leave a message for me on this number, day or night.'

Then he was gone before she could reply, and she could only stand and watch, her head full of angry, disturbing questions, as the low black car U-turned almost at full speed, then accelerated back down the hill again. She frowned down at the small embossed card clutched in her hand. Perhaps, at least, this would tell her who he was.

CHAPTER TWO

'GOOD lord, Jessica, how could you fail to recognise him!' Graham sat back in his seat and smiled in mild astonishment across at her. 'The man's a living legend on the international business scene!'

'I'm sorry, Graham. I'd no idea.' Jessica perched herself on the edge of the counter and threw her fiancé a soothing look. For, beneath his usual unruffled exterior, she could detect an unfamiliar edginess in him and he looked drawn. 'All I knew was that he seemed like the nastiest, most disagreeable individual I'd ever encountered in my entire life.' And that was putting it mildly, she thought.

Graham sighed and tossed the business card the man had given Jessica down on the counter-top in front of him. 'Not to mention undoubtedly the richest and most powerful as well!' He shook his head. 'After all, he's only head of one of the biggest multi-national property companies in Europe, ranked in the top ten in the entire world. Minerva's never out of the news these days. Luke Hartt's face is plastered across the business pages of every damned newspaper you pick up!'

Jessica could have pointed out that she rarely, if ever, scrutinised the business pages. Although, were she in the habit of doing so, she was certain that strong, fiercely commanding face would have branded itself indelibly upon her memory. Instead,

she smoothed the skirt of the red wool dress she'd
changed into over her knees and smiled affectionately across at Graham. 'Well, whoever he is, we
really oughtn't let him get to us, you know.'

'I know. I'm sorry, love.' He shook his head a
trifle wearily and smiled contritely back at her. 'It's
just that it's been such a hell of a day.'

Poor Graham. Jessica reached out kindly and
squeezed his arm. Like her, he'd had a thoroughly
frustrating and upsetting afternoon. Some woman
at the Northampton sale had done to him precisely
what this Luke Hartt individual had done to her—
outbid him on every single item he'd been out to
buy. No wonder he was feeling out of sorts.

She straightened and frowned sympathetically
across at him. 'I'll tell you something else as well.
We've got to stop this man before he starts doing
us some serious damage. We can't just stand meekly
by and let him get away with it.'

'If only it was as easy as that.' Graham's
expression was suddenly grim. 'But people like us
can't stop Luke Hartt, I'm afraid. He's way out of
our league, Jessica. Believe me, that man's so
powerful he can get away with virtually anything.'

Somehow, Jessica had no difficulty at all in believing him. Even without the might and money of
Minerva behind him, Luke Hartt would be a tough
adversary. She made a face. 'But it's not fair. First,
he virtually steals a whole load of merchandise from
under our noses—at a time when it's absolutely
crucial we build up our stock. Then, if your guess
is accurate, he deliberately sets himself up in direct
competition against us.' She nodded meaningfully
in the direction of the shop across the street. For

three months it had stood empty. Now, suddenly, this very afternoon, a notice had appeared in the window: "Opening soon. Spinning Wheel Antiques." 'Do you seriously think that he's behind that, too?'

Graham paused and ran his fingers through his short brown hair. 'I'm absolutely sure of it.' He sighed. 'Normally, I wouldn't even entertain the idea that a giant property company like Minerva could be interested in a tiny, two-bit shop in rural Kent. Five-star hotels on London's Park Lane, multi-million-dollar office blocks—that's more their style. But in the light of what happened this afternoon, and the threats that Luke Hartt made to you, I'd say that a rival opening up directly opposite us is much too much of a coincidence. Hartt has to be behind it.' He shook his head. 'But why? That's what I can't understand.' He fixed his light blue eyes on Jessica. 'What exactly did he say to you?'

Jessica stared down uncomfortably at the floor. 'I told you,' she answered, not quite truthfully, and paused to push the mane of silky, chestnut-coloured hair back from her face. 'He said he intended bringing us to our knees. That was the very expression he used.' But she hadn't told him any of the rest. It would only upset Graham to learn about the nasty, trumped-up accusations that the man had made. And, equally, how could she tell him that Hartt had offered her a personal escape from ruin if she agreed to sell him her share of the business—and left poor Graham in the lurch? Much kinder to keep such squalid details to herself.

'He didn't tell you what his reasons were?' Graham was asking now.

'No.' At least that much was true.

Graham shook his head unhappily. 'The man's a total law unto himself. What hope do we have against someone like that?'

'Maybe none.' Jessica straightened her shoulders belligerently. 'But we can't just let him walk all over us. We've got to fight. That's what I told him, and that's precisely what we're going to do.' And, as though to emphasise her point, she snatched the offending business card from the counter-top and ripped it into tiny shreds. 'That's what I think of his stupid threats! And that's what I think of him! He'll discover he's picked the wrong one to try and bully this time, I promise you!'

'Well said!' Right on cue, Deirdre emerged from the back of the shop with three steaming mugs of coffee on a tray. 'Fighting talk—that's what I like to hear!'

Jessica turned with a smile to the blonde-haired young woman she had come to regard more as a friend than an employee over the past three years. 'We'll show him, won't we?' For she knew that Deirdre was as much a fighter as she herself. Wasn't it Deirdre who'd stood behind her and encouraged her every step of the way through the first two lean and difficult years alone at the helm of Bridge Antiques? Before Graham came on the scene.

She helped herself to a mug of coffee now and took a long, slow, soothing sip. 'This is exactly what I need.' It was the first opportunity she'd had to stop for breath since she'd got back from Tunbridge Wells, what with organising the garage to pick up her abandoned van, and drop off the bureau on the way, then recounting the disasters of the day to

Deirdre and Graham in turn. She'd omitted to
confide in Graham about the *secrétaire*, however,
judging him in no frame of mind to learn that Luke
Hartt had tricked her into paying nearly four
thousand pounds for it. He'd already had more than
enough bad news to cope with for one day.

He had turned with a frown to look at Deirdre
now. 'It's all very well for you to tell Jessica she
should fight,' he informed her reasonably. 'You
don't have anything to lose. If Bridge Antiques goes
under, you can simply go and find yourself another
job.' He paused and turned his gaze, full of
concern, to Jessica. 'For Jessica and me, it's rather
different. Our whole future is at stake.' And he
reached out fondly and took his fiancée's hand in
his. 'Remember, I have to think of that.'

'I know that!' Deirdre bristled visibly at the mild
rebuke. 'And I happen to care as much as you do
about the future of Bridge Antiques,' she snapped.
Then, she added unnecessarily, 'Remember, I've
been involved in the business considerably longer
than you.' And, before he could answer, she turned
away and fixed her gaze on Jessica. 'Are you absolutely sure Hartt didn't give you even the smallest
clue as to why he's doing all this? He must have
said something. Think, Jessica.'

Jessica frowned for a moment and stalled. 'Not
really.' But she had to come up with something.
Two pairs of worried, probing eyes were fixed on
her. On an impulse, she decided to make a small
concession to the truth. 'I got the impression that
he was nursing some kind of grudge.'

'Against us?' Concern cast a sudden shadow over Graham's face. 'What sort of grudge, for heaven's sake?'

'I really don't know,' she shrugged. 'He sort of hinted it might be something personal.' Then she added quickly, to discourage further questioning, 'Of course, we both know that's utterly preposterous. Neither of us has ever had any kind of dealings with the man.'

Graham was frowning thoughtfully into his coffee-cup. 'I'm afraid that's not quite true,' he said at last. 'I've had dealings with him—of a sort. Though it was quite a number of years ago.' And as Jessica blinked, surprised, he added in a sombre tone, 'Rather a nasty incident that I'd long since put to the back of my mind. But I can remember the details all too clearly now.'

He leaned back in his seat and surveyed his fiancée's attentive face. 'It all happened about seven years ago—before Hartt became the big fish he is now. I was working for an antiques dealer in Pimlico—my very first job—and it just so happened that Hartt had recently bought an old three-storey house not very far away from us. Minerva was still a struggling company at the time and Hartt was out to make a nice quick profit on the deal.'

He wagged his head disapprovingly as he went on, 'You see, he'd managed to get the place cheap because there was a sitting tenant on the premises. An old lady who'd lived there all her life. If Hartt could get her to move out, he could resell the property at three times the price he'd paid for it.' He sighed. 'And just in case you have any doubts about what kind of ruthless, inhuman bastard we're dealing with, take note of this. At first, he offered to find the old lady alternative accommodation elsewhere. Then, when she refused to go, he started a vicious campaign of intimidation to force her out. The poor woman was almost out of her mind. I got to hear about the case and, frankly, I was shocked. I knew the maniac had to be stopped.'

Jessica leaned towards him, anticipation mingling with the distaste she felt. 'What did you do?' she asked.

Graham gave a modest smile. 'Not much. I simply reported him to the police, and it was more than his reputation was worth to pursue his vile campaign.'

'Good for you!' Jessica grinned proudly at him. That must have knocked Hartt's arrogant nose out of joint!

He shook his head. 'The trouble is, it looks as though he's never forgiven me for it.'

'You think that's what's behind all this?'

'I'm sure of it.'

'But why would he have waited till now to get even?' Deirdre sounded dubious. 'Wouldn't he have done something long ago?'

'Evidently not.'

There was just a hint of irritation in Graham's voice, and Jessica felt herself tense slightly as Deirdre went on, 'The man's worth millions. It doesn't make sense for him to go on harbouring a grudge over an insignificant financial setback like that.'

She was for ever finding fault with Graham, picking holes in everything he said. And it never failed to upset Jessica.

But Graham seemed to sense the tension in her. He reached out a reassuring hand, as though to tell her he had no intention of allowing himself to be drawn into an argument, then turned with a tolerant smile to the plump-faced woman with the blonde hair. 'Deirdre,' he told her, 'you don't realise what manner of man this Luke Hartt is. He's vindictive and cruel and perfectly capable of harbouring a grudge indefinitely. I promise you, his mind doesn't work like yours or mine.'

'Graham's right.' Instantly, Jessica backed him up. 'The man's not human. It's impossible to judge him according to normal rules.'

Deirdre shrugged. 'Maybe. I suppose you could be right.'

'Unfortunately, we are.' Graham shook his head again. 'And, believe me, Hartt's the last man any sane person would choose for an enemy. He'll stop at nothing—and, with his resources, he can recruit an army against us if it suits his purposes.'

A sudden question occurred to Jessica. 'Who was the woman who kept outbidding you at the Northampton sale? Had you ever seen her before?'

'Not that I can remember. Mind you, she wasn't exactly the sort of woman who stands out in a crowd.'

'What did she look like?'

'Shortish. Dark-haired. Glasses.'

'How old?'

He shrugged. 'It's hard to say. She wasn't young.'

Jessica dismissed an idea that had been forming in her mind. 'In that case, I don't suppose she could have been Hartt's girlfriend. Or his wife.'

'No chance!' Graham discarded the notion with a laugh. 'For one thing, Hartt's not married. Never has been. And I can assure you, his women are invariably young and beautiful. Actresses, models, jet-set types.' He laughed again. 'At least his taste in women is something no one can fault him on.'

Jessica nodded. Yes, that would be true. He no doubt collected desirable females as arbitrarily and cold-bloodedly as he collected antiques.

Graham winked and squeezed her hand. 'But he's yet to land himself one as attractive as you. At least, in that department, I'm one ahead of him.' Then, as Jessica smiled at the compliment, he leaned forward to look intently at her. 'Look, love, I'm truly sorry if I'm the one who's got us into this, but what do you say we try to forget the whole thing just for tonight? I'll treat you to a sumptuous dinner at the restaurant of your choice. Let's just drown our sorrows for a couple of hours.'

'You're on!' Jessica reached out happily and hugged his arm as he turned to Deirdre with a conciliatory smile.

'You come, too,' he told her. Then, as she hesitated, he added persuasively, 'We're all in this together, after all. It's been a rotten day for you as well.'

Deirdre nodded. 'OK.'

Jessica smiled gratefully at him. It was a nice gesture, and somehow typical. For Graham had a knack of smoothing things, of making others feel he had their interests at heart. As she reached up to kiss him affectionately on the cheek, it struck Jessica that agreeing to marry him was probably one of the wisest decisions she'd ever made. His calm assurance was a perfect balance for her own, sometimes rash impetuosity. The two of them would make a perfect pair.

'You're right. To hell with Hartt!' She stood up with a determined smile. 'Let's just live for tonight and let tomorrow take care of itself!'

But tomorrow dawned all too quickly and brought nothing good. Instead, two unfortunate developments occurred. Luke Hartt moved into the Old Mill House, one of the village's grandest and most elegant homes. To use as a weekend retreat, so Jessica heard. And Spinning Wheel Antiques across the road opened for business, leaving no more doubt in anybody's mind that it was part of Luke Hartt's evil scheme.

How could it be anything else? Every single item that Jessica and Graham had bid for on that fateful afternoon was on sale—and at prices that could only be described as ludicrous. The roll-top desk Luke Hartt had bought for nine hundred pounds now bore a price tag of three hundred and fifty. The little mahogany side table that cost him five hundred was on offer now for a mere two hundred and twenty-five.

And the story was the same throughout the shop, as Deirdre was able to report after a quick spying trip one afternoon. Jessica was being undercut on a scale that could only spell disaster for Bridge Antiques.

The ginger-haired young man in charge merely shrugged when Deirdre tried to question him. 'Some pretty good bargains, don't you think?' he offered with a guileless smile.

The buying public evidently thought so. As word got round, trade across the street boomed almost embarrassingly, while the takings at Bridge Antiques plummeted to a disastrous all-time low. In a desperate effort to compete, Jessica slashed her prices to the barest minimum. But she couldn't go on doing that indefinitely and hope to survive.

'Another couple of months like this and we're in serious trouble,' she confided bitterly to Deirdre, as they counted the scanty takings after their fourth dismal weekend. And she clenched her fist and banged it down hard on the counter-top. The situation was intolerable. It was as though the very bedrock of her security was being torn right out from under her.

Abruptly, she got to her feet and crossed to the window. She stood there for a moment, glowering across the street. 'First thing tomorrow morning,' she vowed, 'I intend to pay Luke Hartt a little visit and inform him he's gone too far with this vendetta of his.' She squared her shoulders decisively. 'If Graham wants to come with me, well and good. If not, I'll go and speak to that infernal bully by myself!'

Next morning, just before nine, Jessica took the van and drove, unaccompanied, to the Old Mill House. A sprawling half-timbered mansion dating from the eighteenth century, it stood well back from the road, amid fifteen or so acres of woodland, flowerbeds and endlessly stretching lawns. It was far too beautiful a place for an inhuman monster like Luke Hartt, she reflected drily as she parked the van under some trees. But at least he was home.

The sleek black Porsche was parked just a few yards away. Now she would beard the lion in his den.

Taking a deep breath, she marched up to the oak front door and banged the brass knocker with all her strength. She was just on the point of banging it again when, abruptly, the door was pulled open and she found herself staring into a woman's gaunt, unsmiling face.

'Yes?' She was short, bespectacled, middle-aged. Not the sort of woman who would stand out in a crowd.

Jessica stepped forward. 'I've come to see Mr Hartt,' she said.

The woman peered back at her through narrowed eyes. 'Do you have an appointment?' she asked.

'No, but if you'll just tell him that Jessica Langley of Bridge Antiques would like to talk to him, I'm sure he'll manage to find a minute or two.'

The woman shook her head and took a step back, away from her. 'I'm sorry, but Mr Hartt is extremely busy right now. He's not seeing anyone.' And, to Jessica's horror, she began to close the door.

'Hey, hang on! Not so fast!' Without pausing to think, Jessica jumped forward and forced the door wide, ignoring the startled, outraged expression on the other woman's face. 'I'm afraid I have to see him. It's very important!' She glanced quickly round the opulently furnished hall in which she suddenly found herself. 'Now, if you wouldn't mind telling me where he is?'

The woman glared at her. 'He's in his study. But I've already told you he's not to be disturbed.'

'You may as well show me to his study now. I'm not leaving till I've spoken to him.' Jessica was adamant.

The woman's thin lips tightened stubbornly, but her eyes darted betrayingly to a door at the far end of the hall. And, before she could reach out a hand to stop her tall, green-eyed intruder, Jessica was striding across the thick-pile carpet towards her goal. Then, without even bothering to knock, she pushed the door open and stepped inside.

He was seated behind a large mahogany desk, and at the sight of her a look of intense irritation flashed across his face. Very slowly, he rose to his feet. 'And to what do I owe this intrusion?' he enquired, an unmistakable edge of menace in the deep, dark voice. 'Tell me, Miss Langley, do you make a habit of barging into other people's homes?'

It was the first time she had seen him standing, and he was even taller than she had supposed, the harsh, dark lines of the sunbronzed face even more commanding than she recalled. He was dressed for riding, in finely cut jodhpurs and high leather boots that emphasised the muscular strength of the long, lean calves, while the pale yellow cashmere crewneck sweater that he wore hugged the taut lines of his shoulders and chest.

'I couldn't stop her, Mr Hartt.' The woman with the spectacles had positioned herself between Jessica and the desk in a gesture that was touchingly, if superfluously, protective. Luke Hartt needed protecting from nobody. 'She just pushed past me. Very nearly knocked me down.'

'Yes, Miss Clutton, I'm sure she did.' The grey eyes were hard with disapproval, the fine lips drawn into an unrelenting line. 'But, don't worry, I'll deal with her now.'

Flush-faced, Jessica stood there in the middle of the room, confronting him, as, with evident reluctance and a final outraged glance at her, the dutiful Miss Clutton left the room. So he thought he was going to deal with her, did he? Well, he had that the wrong way round! Boldly, she stepped forward and, without waiting to be invited, seated herself opposite him in a crimson, velvet-upholstered wingback chair. 'I think you know why I'm here, Mr Hartt. I've come to protest in the strongest possible terms at the lowdown, dirty way you're trying to put me out of business.' And she reached up to toss an errant strand of glossy, chestnut-coloured hair back from her face.

He sat down in his seat again and folded strong brown arms across his chest. 'Frankly, I don't give a damn what brings you here. But I'll tell you one thing, your protests are a waste of time.'

She winced at the cold, dismissive tone of voice. Did he, perhaps, expect her just to get up and go? Well, he was in for an unpleasant shock. 'I trust you will nevertheless have the grace at least to hear me out?'

He glanced down at his watch and shrugged. 'If you don't object to wasting your time, I suppose I can spare you a couple of minutes or so.'

'Good.' She injected all the sarcasm that she could into the single syllable and squared her shoulders before going on. 'I take it I'm correct in assuming that Spinning Wheel Antiques belongs to you?'

He raised a disdainful black eyebrow at her. 'To Minerva, to be precise.'

'It's the same thing, isn't it, since you happen to be the sole shareholder in that particular company?' She'd been doing a lot of homework over the past few weeks. 'So what does a company the size of Minerva want with a little antiques shop in Harbingdon?'

A smile curved at the corner of his lips. 'Let's just say, I felt inclined to dabble in antiques.'

So he was making fun of her! Angry colour flooded into her face, and she clenched her fists into hard, tight balls. 'I'm afraid I don't think it's funny, Mr Hartt. This vicious little game of yours is literally crippling me. If you keep it up, I'll be lucky to last the summer out.'

He leaned back his head and looked across at her, his expression parodying sympathy. 'That's a great pity,' he observed. Then glanced at his desktop, seeming to ponder her remark. 'Are you seriously trying to tell me that your business could go under in a matter of months?'

Jessica nodded, her expression intent. Perhaps he hadn't realised how serious the situation was for her. Perhaps, now, he might be moved to take a more compassionate stand.

'Well, well.' The grey eyes snapped up to lock with hers again. 'That's even sooner than I'd hoped.'

The unexpected cruelty of his observation hit her like a body blow. 'What do you mean?' she gasped.

He threw her a callous look. 'I wouldn't have thought that was a particularly obscure remark. But if you want me to spell it out to you, it means that

I'd reckoned it would probably take till the end of the year before I had the satisfaction of seeing you and your boyfriend quietly fold up your tents and steal off ignominiously into the night.'

'That will never happen!' Her fingers clutched at the arm of the chair, knuckles white, and she stared across at him through hate-filled eyes. 'This is my home. If you're trying to drive me out of Harbingdon, you'll never succeed!'

'That, dear Jessica, remains to be seen.' He spoke the endearment with a cruel twist of his mouth that made the hairs on the back of Jessica's neck stand up. 'I warned you. I gave you the chance to get out while the going was good. But it's too late now. If you choose to stand by that charlatan—as you have amply demonstrated that you intend to do—then that, I'm afraid, is your funeral. And don't think about moving to another town and starting up another little business there. I'll only follow you. And I'll drive the pair of you out again—wherever you go!'

'I've already told you, I'm not going anywhere!' Her heart was thudding dully inside her breast. 'This is my home, Mr Hartt, and this is where I intend to stay.' She swallowed hard. 'I think you're behaving despicably. What you're doing is totally out of proportion to what Graham did to you— and he had every right to do what he did.' Then, seeing the sudden interest in his eyes. 'Yes, I know what's behind this malicious vendetta of yours, and I think it's shameful. But it just goes to illustrate even more what an unscrupulous bully you are!'

The expression in the dark grey eyes was quizzical. 'What an unscrupulous bully *I* am? I would have thought that was a more fitting description for that boyfriend of yours.'

'Don't try to fob me off with any more lies. I know what you tried to do to that poor old lady in Pimlico!'

He gave her a blank look. 'My dear Miss Langley, I haven't a clue what you're talking about. What poor old lady in Pimlico?'

Jessica took a deep breath before going on. So he intended to disclaim the shady dealings in his past, did he? The man was even more despicable than she had thought. 'You don't deny that about seven years ago you bought a house in Pimlico?' she asked.

'I don't deny it.'

'And living in that house was an old lady, a sitting tenant who'd been there for years and whom you attempted to intimidate into leaving, in order that you could sell the house at a huge profit.'

A totally unreadable expression settled on his face. 'Continue,' was all he said.

So, he didn't deny it! Jessica went on eagerly, 'My fiancé discovered what you were up to and reported you to the police, so that you were forced to abandon your vile campaign. He did you out of a nice, fat profit and you've never forgiven him for it. That's why you're trying to make him pay for it now.' She leaned forward and scrutinised his face. 'Isn't that so, Mr Hartt?'

For a long, strained moment, he said not a word. Then, totally unexpectedly, he threw back his head and laughed. A rich and resonant laugh, amused and somehow derisive at the same time. 'So that's what he's been telling you,' he said at last. And his lips curled contemptuously as he went on, 'My dear Miss Langley, do you really believe everything that scoundrel tells you?'

Jessica was totally taken aback. This was not the reaction she had expected at all. 'Are you trying to tell me it isn't true?' But she knew that he was bluffing, of course.

'It's sheer and utter fabrication from start to finish. Cole is the one who specialises in ripping off old ladies—not me.' He paused, the dark eyes coldly scrutinising her face. 'But then, I suspect you're already aware of that and have chosen, for reasons of your own, to conveniently overlook the fact. In my eyes, that makes you as guilty as him.'

Before he could say another word, Jessica cut in, 'I didn't come here to listen to your lies and your threats. I came here, quite simply, to inform you that I know what's *really* behind this vendetta of yours.' She took a deep breath and looked him straight in the eye. 'And to ask you to call it off.'

He leaned back slowly in his seat, surveying her, and there was not a grain of compassion in the gold-flecked eyes. 'So why didn't Cole come with you to plead his case?'

'I didn't come to plead.' Her spine stiffened defensively at the word. 'Just to try and reason with you. And Graham wasn't able to accompany me because he was tied up with important business elsewhere.'

'How convenient.'

'And what is that supposed to mean?'

He leaned forward, his strong arms folded on the desk in front of him. 'I don't suppose the real reason could be that he was afraid to come?'

A flush of indignation rose at once to Jessica's cheeks. 'And why should he be afraid of you?' she demanded angrily.

He shrugged and sat back in his seat again. 'Ask him.' Then, lacing the fingers of his lean brown hands together, he rested the knuckles thoughtfully against his chin. 'Whatever possessed you to hand over fifty per cent of your business to that character?' he enquired, completely changing the subject. 'I understand you were doing very nicely on your own.'

Jessica glared at him. Why, the impertinence! 'If it's any business of yours—which it is not!—Graham has contributed a great deal to Bridge Antiques over the past twelve months. He deserved to have a share in it.'

He gave a short, derisive little laugh. 'Fifty per cent sounds like extremely generous remuneration for one year's work.'

She met his gaze with more than equal derision of her own. What would he know about generosity? Besides, he had no damned right to comment on her private affairs! 'I see nothing generous about it,' she snapped. 'Graham and I love each other and plan to marry soon. It's only right that we should share things equally.'

'And, no doubt, he has lavished fifty per cent of all his worldly possessions on you in return?'

She glared at him, resenting the mockery in his voice. Resenting somehow, even more, the niggling truth that the remark contained. When it came to the lavishing of worldly goods, Graham, so far, had been notably restrained. Even the money he had agreed to pay her for his fifty per cent, barring a small deposit, was outstanding still, though he had assured her there was a perfectly good reason for that, and she was certainly too loyal to admit it now. 'Graham and I are perfectly happy with the way we have our lives arranged, so you really needn't concern yourself.'

He smiled a slow and somehow irritating smile. 'I can see how the arrangement might suit Cole. I understand your generosity even extends to providing a roof over his head?'

Jessica straightened angrily in her seat. Well, that piece of calumny was definitely wrong! 'As a matter of fact,' she retorted drily, 'I live alone in the flat above the shop. My fiancé rents rooms in Harbingdon.'

A flicker of amusement momentarily softened the harsh lines of Hartt's face. 'How very unsatisfactory for both of you. And particularly for Cole, if I may say so.' His gaze shifted pointedly to the firm, high breasts beneath the simple sweater that she wore, the long, slender curves of the shapely thighs, outlined against the fabric of her jeans. And in that single, penetrating glance, he seemed to ravish her with his eyes. 'If I had a fiancée who looked like you, I'd find such an arrangement quite intolerable.'

Jessica fought back the sudden colour that was flooding her cheeks. 'Fortunately, not all men are animals!' she spat.

He laughed then, openly enjoying the discomfort he had provoked in her. 'Surely you don't believe that a man's natural impulse to make love to a beautiful woman makes him an animal?'

'There are such qualities as restraint and respect for one's partner,' she reminded him tightly. 'Qualities I would naturally not expect a man like you to possess. I'm happy to say that my fiancé does.'

He glanced across at her with a taunting smile. 'My condolences,' he said.

He was hateful. Arrogant. Cruel. And totally without morality.

'I wonder,' she put to him, acid dripping from her every syllable, 'were you actually born this nasty, or did you have to work at it?'

He shook his head and smiled a villain's smile. 'Believe me, Jessica, all of my assets were hard-won.' Then, abruptly, he got to his feet, glancing at his watch. 'I'm going for a ride now. If you wish to continue your interrogation, you'll have to do it on horseback, I'm afraid.'

Jessica frowned up at him. What the devil was he up to now?

'As you can see——' he indicated the jodhpurs and riding boots he wore '—I was just about to go out riding when you so rudely interrupted me.' Then, in a couple of strides, he came round the desk and stood towering over her like some magnificent dark Lucifer.

She flinched away, uncomfortably conscious of his proximity, and debated whether to take this opportunity to end a confrontation that was getting her precisely nowhere, after all. So far, her trip had been an indisputable waste of time. But she was reluctant to throw in the towel so easily. Perhaps there was still some way to persuade this man to abandon his evil campaign. Yet accepting to go for a ride with him felt uncomfortably like fraternising with the enemy. 'Couldn't we continue our conversation here?'

He glanced down at her with a wicked smile. 'What's the matter, Jessica?' he challenged. 'Are you afraid of being alone with me, out of earshot of the domestic help?' Then he added with a frown, 'I take it you do know how to ride?'

'I'm not an expert, but I can ride—and I've already told you, Mr Hartt, I'm not afraid of you.' Lest he double it, she stood up quickly, resisting the impulse to take a step away from him. 'If it will amuse you, I'll come along.' At least, in her jeans and sweater, she was dressed for it. And it might just provide the perfect opportunity to catch the great Luke Hartt off guard.

Miss Clutton was poised in the hallway, almost as though she'd been waiting for them to appear. 'Are you going for your ride now, Mr Hartt?' she enquired, throwing Jessica a smile as winsome as an armoured tank.

Hartt nodded. 'That's right, Miss Clutton. And Miss Langley will be accompanying me. Give Jack a ring at the stables,' he instructed, 'and tell him to saddle up the grey as well.' Then he turned to Jessica with an unfathomable smile. 'He's a spirited young stallion. He should suit you well.'

'Will that be all, Mr Hartt?' Again the quick dart of hostility at Jessica as, reluctantly, she stood aside.

'Yes, thank you, Miss Clutton.' Then, over his shoulder to Jessica 'We'll go out the back way. Follow me.'

She almost had to run to keep up with him, as he led her through the warren of corridors that led to the back of the house. Corridors hung with vivid oils and bright with the sudden colour of a bowl of flowers. Corridors that afforded her sharp eyes the occasional brief glimpse through some open door into the room beyond—and simultaneously into the dark, mysterious psyche of the owner of the house. From the strong, simple statements of the décor, she could sense that he was a man of deep-felt convictions, a singular individual who followed to the beat of no man's drum. But unpredictable as well, she felt, as some unexpected, idiosyncratic detail caught her eye. Full of powerful, dark forces and untamed desires.

Outside in the paved backyard, a Land Rover was waiting for them. He opened the passenger door. 'We'll drive. It's quicker.' He climbed in beside her and gunned the engine. 'You've made a very bad impression on my secretary, I fear.' And allowed himself a quick flash of a smile.

'Miss Clutton? Your self-appointed guard dog, from the look of things! And a woman of many talents—as my fiancé had occasion to observe at a certain Northampton sale only the other week.' She turned to look at him with dry censure as they moved away. 'Tell me, how many people do you employ to do your dirty work for you?'

Amusement flickered in the dark-tanned face. 'Just as many as I need. But, don't worry, they're all handsomely paid.'

Jessica threw him a disparaging look. 'Money isn't everything, you know.'

'I'm glad to hear you say so.' A note of amused sadism sounded in his voice. 'If I may say so, coming from someone like yourself, on the brink of financial ruin, I find that a truly admirable philosophy.'

God, he could be cruel! She swung round to fix him with accusing green eyes. 'You really enjoy it, don't you, Hartt? It pleases you no end to watch your fellows suffering. You're not even human!'

He disdained to meet her eyes and his tone was coolly dismissive as he replied, 'Knowing your own and your boyfriend's standards of humanity, I take that as a compliment.'

Jack, the head groom, was waiting for them at the stables. 'Rabindrath is ready for you, Mr Hartt.' Then, with a distinctly curious glance in the direction of Jessica, 'And Looking-Glass'll be ready for the young lady in a tick.'

'Good. Miss Langley can borrow Miss Clutton's hard hat and boots. They ought to fit.'

They did, more or less, though Jessica couldn't help feeling just a shade peculiar as she pulled on the dragon's attire. Any minute now she'd start breathing fire! But all such frivolous thoughts were swept from her mind as Jack appeared leading a magnificent black stallion—Rabindrath, Luke Hartt's mount, she guessed—with, right behind him and towering over the stable lad who led him out, broad-chested, strong flanks quivering expectantly, Looking-Glass, her own mount, a handsome grey. A sudden sharp excitement burned in her breast. She'd never ridden anything like this before!

'Like him?' Luke Hartt was watching her.

'He's beautiful.' She nodded, and smiled as the boy handed her the reins.

'Good. Let's go, then.' Luke Hartt waited for her to mount.

She put her left foot in the stirrup and simultaneously reached for the saddle—but before she could lift herself up on to the horse's back, Hartt had caught her by the ankle to steady her, his grip firm and oddly disconcerting in its easy familiarity. A flush of irritation flamed her face. She neither needed nor wanted his help. Not that he gave a damn about her, she reminded herself, as, without even glancing up at her, he expertly adjusted the stirrup straps. His concern, undoubtedly, was for the well-being of the horse.

He moved away to his own mount, Rabindrath, and swung himself up into the saddle with easy grace. And it struck her as he turned away, moving ahead of her, that there was something splendidly beautiful, even majestic, in the vision presented by man and beast. Two proud, dark creatures moving as one, their separate strengths pooled in the creation of a greater, more powerful harmony.

He turned to check that she was following. 'He needs a firm hand,' he advised. Then amended hurriedly, 'Not too firm,' as she dug her heels overzealously into the horse's flanks, making him skitter forward nervously. 'Just let him know who's boss, that's all.'

They rode at a gentle trot for a couple of miles, in a silence that was almost companionable. Hartt came alongside her presently. 'OK? Enjoying yourself?'

She nodded. 'Yes, thanks.' But she hadn't come along just to enjoy herself. She had come to try and subtly twist his arm. It wasn't in her nature to beg, but if a bit of strategic cajoling would do the trick, she was prepared to try. She smiled at him. She would make her move when he showed himself a little more amenable.

He led her down past the wood and along the bridle path across rough fields—and as they rode she found herself casting the occasional, curious glance at him. Somewhere behind that hard, implacable exterior, a tiny spark of human compassion must burn. She must find it and use it to her advantage while there was still time.

At the top of the rise, he paused to look round at the rich green rolling hills of the Kent countryside, breathing in deeply the clean, clear air. 'Yes,' he murmured to himself, almost as though he'd forgotten she was there, 'I could really grow to love this place.'

'I already do.' Perhaps this was the moment she'd been waiting for. 'I know that it would break my heart if I had to leave.'

He swivelled round to look at her, his tone suddenly coldly matter-of-fact. 'Then dump Cole and accept my offer to buy you out. I'm prepared to give you one last chance.'

'Never! Why can't you just forget this stupid grudge of yours, and leave my fiancé and me in peace?'

He gave her a long look and, just for a moment or two, it seemed to Jessica that she could detect a flicker of uncertainty in the hard grey eyes. Suddenly hopeful, she pressed her point.

'We've already suffered enough. We don't deserve what you're doing to us.'

'No, you don't.' He took a deep breath. 'You deserve a great deal worse. And I intend to see that that's exactly what you get.'

It was as though he had slapped her to her senses. Appealing for mercy from a man like him was as futile as trying to coax sunbeams out of cucumbers. Proudly, she straightened in the saddle and faced up to him. 'You're not going to succeed, you know! I've already told you that I'll fight you, and I will!'

He laughed nastily. 'A waste of time, dear Jessica, I promise you.' His eyes were as merciless as an executioner's. 'You are already existing on borrowed time.'

Suddenly, she could no longer bear to look at him. With a furious jerk, she turned Looking-Glass's head away and dug her heels impatiently into his flanks. 'To hell with you! I'm going back!'

As she pulled impatiently at the reins, the horse whinnied in protest and reared back. And it was just as she was struggling to regain control that, somewhere in the woods, just a short distance away from them, the sharp crack of a rifle rang out. It was fearfully mistimed. The horse seemed to freeze for a moment in mid-air, then lunged forward wildly, bolting at full stretch back down the hill.

'Stop!' she screamed. But there was no stopping him. In a desperate effort to hang on, she threw herself across his shoulders, clutching frantically at his mane, feeling the breath knocked from her body as he pounded, gathering speed, across the flat. Then a spasm of horror gripped her as she realised her right foot had come free from the stirrup and she was sliding, sliding. And all she could see were the thundering hooves, the dry green turf as it streaked by beneath her, closer and ever closer now.

And she closed her eyes as the sickening certainty gripped her that, any second, she was going to fall.

What a way to go, she reflected with bitter irony through her fear. Trampled to a bloody death beneath the hooves of one of Luke Hartt's stallions!

CHAPTER THREE

'HERE, Jessica! Grab hold of me!'

A strong hand suddenly seized her by the arm, wrenching her upwards, just as it seemed she was about to hit the ground. And through her blind terror she was dimly aware of a powerful, dark presence galloping at her side, and an overwhelming sense of relief rushed through her as, in that instant, she realised she was not going to die.

'Hold tight.'

Only half aware of her responses, she somehow summoned the will to respond to his command. She reached out and clung with all her feeble strength to the arm that had wrapped itself firmly around her middle and was hauling her bodily across the gap that divided the two steeds, lifting her tall, slender frame as though she were a weightless doll and setting her down on the smooth, firm saddle between his thighs.

He held the reins of both stallions in his free hand now, forcing the runaway grey to slow, first to a canter, then, finally, to a gentle trot. 'Are you all right?'

She nodded, still too dazed and breathless to speak. She had come within a whisker of probable death and almost certain horrible injury, and he had snatched her to safety just in time. He was the last man in the world she might ever have expected to feel grateful to, but she felt deeply grateful to him now.

'We'll get you back to the house, young lady.' His breath was warm against her hair. 'A stiff brandy's what you need.'

Jessica remembered nothing of the ride back to the stables with Luke. Nothing, that was, except the almost overpowering nearness of him. The warmth of his broad chest pressing against her back, the hard, restraining strength of his muscular thighs. And the fact that, surprisingly, that nearness was reassuring somehow.

There was a flurry of concern among Jack and the lads at the stables when they got back. 'Is she hurt?' she dimly heard one of them ask.

'I don't think so.' Luke dismounted quickly, while Jack helped her to the ground. 'But I'll get Doc Bingham to take a look at her back at the house.' Then, when she stumbled drunkenly as she attempted to take a step, he whisked her into his arms and carried her to the Land Rover.

'I'm sorry,' she murmured, faintly embarrassed by her unaccustomed state of helplessness. 'I guess I'm still a bit shaky.' The truth was, her legs felt like cotton wool, her whole body numb and aching at the same time, as though it had been used as a punching bag.

'Don't apologise. It's all my fault.' His face was grim, with a mixture of annoyance and concern, as he settled her in the passenger seat and came round to the other side. 'I should never have allowed you to ride that horse. He's far too highly strung. But I thought if I kept an eye on you, you'd be all right.' He scowled with annoyance that was clearly directed principally at himself. 'I hadn't reckoned on some damned poacher scaring the living daylights out of him.'

'How could you?' Jessica shot him an understanding glance. 'Don't blame yourself. It was just one of those things. Just a silly accident.'

'Maybe.' He swung the Land Rover out on to the narrow track that led back to the Old Mill House. 'But you were with me on my property. I'm afraid that makes you my responsibility. I have no choice but to accept the blame.'

Jessica glanced across at the strong, dark profile of the man at her side with a sense of bemused curiosity. What a bewildering confusion of contrasts he was! One minute, he was all menacing anger and threats, not caring that he was bound on a course that was destined to destroy her utterly. The next, he was expressing concern over what, in the event, was only a minor accident, and regret over his small part in it. But he was definitely wrong in one assumption. She put him right.

'I'm nobody's responsibility, Mr Hartt—and very definitely not yours.' Over the years, since both her parents had died, she'd grown used to fending for herself and relying on her own resources above all else. Even Graham's arrival on the scene had not changed that. 'I'm perfectly able to look after myself.'

An amused smile flitted across the dark-tanned face. 'I'm afraid I've had precious little evidence of that so far. From what I've seen, I'd say that quite the opposite's the case.'

She glared at him. 'It may appear to you as if I spend all of my time falling off horses and suffering mechanical breakdowns in the rain—not to mention allowing myself to get ripped off at auction sales. But, in between all that, I manage to run a more-than-moderately successful little business. At least, I did until you came along.'

'If you say so.' He brought the Land Rover to a halt on the gravel driveway at the back of the house, climbed out and flicked her a perfunctory glance as she started to open up her door. 'Stay where you are. I'll give you a hand. I don't want you collapsing on me again.'

In spite of an overwhelming urge to defy him, Jessica remained obediently in her seat. It went totally against the grain to fall in with the commands that this man so easily handed out to her. But, just for the moment, she had the feeling he knew best.

'Here, take my arm.' He came round to her side and helped her out. And it was true, she did still feel a bit wobbly—though she kept her grip on his arm as light as possible. There was something almost too intimate about any form of physical contact with him. Something oddly powerful and vaguely disquieting. And she kept her eyes fixed straight ahead as they crossed the short distance to the door and he guided her through a maze of corridors to a big, sunny room at the front of the house.

Miss Clutton appeared in the doorway just as he was helping Jessica into a chair. Dark beams of hostility shone from her narrowed eyes. 'You're back very early, Mr Hartt. Is something wrong?'

He turned and raised his dark grey eyes to her. 'I'm afraid Miss Langley has had a bit of an accident. Perhaps you'd be good enough to give Dr Bingham a call and ask him to come out here immediately?'

'Nothing serious, I hope?' The thin, bespectacled woman lifted an eyebrow questioningly, but there was none of the compassion of her words reflected in the tone in which she uttered them. She sounded merely irked and more than a little sceptical, as though she suspected that Jessica had deliberately engineered this little incident to draw attention and sympathy to herself.

'No, nothing serious,' Hartt responded. 'Really just a nasty shock. But I'd like Bingham to come out and take a look at her, anyway.'

'Very well, Mr Hartt.'

As Miss Clutton started to move away, Jessica turned protestingly towards Hartt. 'I'm perfectly all right, you know. You needn't go to all this trouble on my account.'

'What trouble?' He waved her protestations aside. 'Please, Miss Langley, don't make a fuss.' Then, crossing to the drinks cabinet at the far end of the room, he lifted out a bottle of Rémy Martin and two brandy balloons. 'While we're waiting, I think a drop of this won't do you any harm.' And he proceeded to pour two generous measures.

Jessica glanced curiously around the room. It was evidently one of the Old Mill House's main reception rooms, an airy, elegant room of generous proportions, furnished in a highly individual mix of antique English and modern-day Italian, mellow oak and mahogany blending comfortably with supple leather and the sharp sheen of chrome. A room of strength and character, full of sharply defined contrasts and cleverly construed effects. Much like the owner of the house, she observed to herself.

'Here. Drink this slowly.' He sat down opposite her and smiled ruefully as he raised his own glass to his lips. 'I hope you don't mind if I join you? I don't usually drink at this early hour—but you're not the only one who's had a fright.'

And it struck her, as she took a mouthful of the fiery cognac and let it trickle slowly down her throat, that it was the first time she had ever seen him smile. Really smile. For there was an uncharacteristically unguarded quality about him now, almost as though, because of the accident, he had decided, temporarily, to suspend hostilities. She sat back in her seat and shook her head as the paradox of the situation occurred to her. 'I must say, when I came here this morning, the last thing I expected was that I would end up sitting here drinking brandy with you.' She smiled a wry smile. 'What a pity there isn't really anything to celebrate.'

He fixed her with a dark, impenetrable eye. 'Champagne is for celebrations, not cognac. Besides——' he drained his glass and laid it abruptly to one side '—I would have thought that emerging from that little escapade back there with all your limbs intact would have been cause enough for celebration if you needed one. I thought at one point I was going to have to carry you back here in bits.'

She threw him a bitter smile. 'Don't try to tell me you wouldn't have derived a certain pleasure from that.'

'Not in the slightest.' He sat back and casually hooked one boot-clad ankle over the opposite knee.

'I hate to see unnecessary waste. And, anyway, I'm not really the sadist you seem to think I am.'

Somehow, Jessica was not quite ready to believe that yet. She threw him a disdainful smile. 'If I may quote: "I'm afraid I've had precious little evidence of that so far."'

He smiled. 'A pity.' And regarded her provocatively through lowered lids. 'I think in other, more favourable circumstances, I might have quite enjoyed showing you my more positive side.'

'Dr Bingham is on his way.' Miss Clutton was hovering in the doorway again.

'Good. Thank you.' His eyes still fixed on Jessica, Hartt nodded an acknowledgement. The woman retreated, but not without first delivering a warning glance at Jessica. And, as the door closed behind her again, it struck Jessica that, as Graham had said, Hartt probably had an army of such hostile individuals working for him. All handsomely paid, of course, and more than willing to do his dirty work for him. She glanced across at him with renewed dislike.

'I doubt very much that you have a positive side,' she told him coldly. 'And I doubt there's anything about you I could possibly have pleasure finding out.'

'In that case,' he conceded, still holding her eyes and flashing an insolent smile at her, 'the pleasure would have been all mine.'

The doctor arrived and pronounced Jessica perfectly recovered from her accident. 'You've had a nasty shock,' he told her. 'Best take it easy for a couple of days.'

'So there's nothing to stop me leaving here now.'
Jessica started to get to her feet the moment the
doctor had gone.

'Not so fast, Jessica. Just stay where you are.'
Hartt was on his feet as well, one firm, restraining
hand held out in front of her. 'Don't think for one
second I'd allow you to drive back in the state
you're in.'

'I don't need your permission!' She was rapidly
growing rather tired of the way he kept ordering
her about.

He ignored the protest and, in a couple of strides,
crossed over to the telephone. 'What's the number
of Bridge Antiques?' he demanded, picking up the
receiver.

She told him, then added suspiciously, 'What do
you want it for?'

He quickly punched the numbers in and lifted
the receiver to his ear. 'I think it's only proper that
your boyfriend should come round and collect you,
don't you? Besides——' he threw her a subversive
smile '—it's a splendid opportunity for us to meet.'

Jessica stared back dully at him. Did he have to
seek out a confrontation with Graham as well? That
was the last thing she wanted now. As it was,
Graham had been far from enthusiastic about her
coming here, claiming that she would only end up
making matters worse. Hartt, he had counselled
her, was a man from whom it was wise to stay as
far away as possible. He was hardly likely to thank
her now for having him lured into the lion's den.

She sat back stiffly in her chair and said nothing,
putting up a silent prayer that Graham had still not
returned from his errand in Canterbury. But it was

not to be. A moment later, she cringed inwardly as she heard Hartt bark out a couple of sharp commands down the phone—did it never occur to the man that others perhaps did not appreciate being spoken to that way? Graham, she knew, most certainly would not. There was absolutely nothing more guaranteed to anger him.

Hartt laid down the receiver and walked back slowly across the room. 'He's coming, you'll be pleased to hear.' Although he was perfectly well aware that she was very far from pleased. 'He says he'll have to walk, so he may be a little while.' He regarded her thoughtfully for a moment as he sat down. 'Don't worry. Though it will be an immense effort, I shall endeavour to be civil to him. You've had more than enough upset for the day.' And he leaned back in his chair and stretched his long legs out in front of him. 'So, Jessica, what shall we talk about till he arrives?'

She glared across at him resentfully. Why did he always have to be the one in the driver's seat? 'If you don't mind, I'd just as soon talk about nothing,' she replied.

'That would be very boring, don't you think?' The grey eyes surveyed her with mocking amusement in their steely depths. 'Let's talk about you, Jessica. Tell me all about yourself.'

She shot him an abrasive smile. 'I thought you already knew all about me, Mr Hartt. Isn't that what you told me the first time we met?'

He shook his head. 'Not *all*. A great deal, is what I said. And I'm slightly curious about the gaps.'

'Are you? How very perverse!' Impatiently, the green eyes locked with his. 'You like to know all about your victims, do you, before you deliver the *coup de grâce*? I thought it was supposed to be easier for the executioner if his victims remained anonymous. But I suppose for someone with the practice you've had it simply adds flavour to the job.'

He completely ignored her taunt. 'I know that you were born and brought up in Hereford, and that you moved south to London about five years ago.'

So he'd been digging back into her past, trespassing into her private affairs. She straightened aggressively. 'I moved south when my parents died. They were killed in an air crash when I was eighteen.' Then she added accusingly, 'But I suppose you already knew that, too.'

He nodded. 'Yes, I did, as a matter of fact. And I'm sorry.'

'Sorry!' she scoffed. 'Why should you be sorry?'

'Because I think it's a tragedy to lose one's parents so young.'

The remark was spoken with apparent sincerity, and she even thought she saw a spark of understanding in the hard grey eyes. Perhaps that was why she found herself adding, in a somewhat milder tone of voice, 'After they were killed, I had nothing to keep me in Hereford. I thought I'd make a better living if I moved south.'

'Didn't you have any other family?'

So there were a couple of things he didn't know! 'None close. A couple of cousins, but they're much older than me. I hardly knew them.' She shook the chestnut hair back from her face and smiled, more to herself, really, than to him. 'My parents had me very late, you see, and I missed out on all the brothers and sisters and cousins bit. I do actually have a sister, but we've never even met. She'd already married and emigrated to Australia before I was born.'

'That's a shame. I think you missed out.' He ran one finger down the side of his long, straight nose. 'I think every child should grow up in a big family.'

'I take it, in that case, that you did?' She would hardly have judged him much of a recommendation for large families. Or for anything else, come to that.

'There were six of us. Four boys, two girls—and I couldn't even begin to count the number of cousins we had.'

Well, given the law of averages, she supposed they couldn't all have turned out as badly as him.

'I was the youngest,' he informed her before she could ask. 'A bit of a rebel, I'm afraid——' so he was the black sheep, after all! '—and the only one out of the six of us who didn't follow our father into law.'

She frowned at him. The renegade son. 'No doubt you rejected the concepts of justice and fair play at an early age. The law would have been a most unfitting occupation for someone with your turn of mind.'

He deliberately chose to misunderstand. 'You're probably right. Like my brothers and sisters, I took a degree in law, but I found I needed a little more personal challenge in my career. I liked the idea of starting out from base alone, of building up something from nothing on the strength of my own instincts and abilities. Something real and tangible that I could point to as my own. I bought my first piece of property—a terrace of run-down houses in Lewisham, before the area became fashionable— with a loan from my father. And he had every single penny of it, plus interest, back within five years.'

How touching! She sniffed. 'And according to the Press cuttings, you were a millionaire before you were thirty.'

'Long before.'

'And how many people did you have to step on and put out of business on your way?' Her tone was dismissive, hard. 'Please don't think for one minute that I admire people like you, Mr Hartt.'

He smiled an irritating smile. 'People who bully old ladies in Pimlico, you mean?'

'I don't think that's funny, even if you do.' Jessica sat forward in her seat and peered total condemnation at him. 'I know that to the great boss of Minerva, the small man or woman doesn't matter in the least. We're just here to be bullied and taken advantage of.' She took a deep breath and fought to control the anger rising in her. 'I've no doubt your path is littered with casualties like the little old lady in Pimlico—and others that you like to laugh about.' She glared at him. 'Including me.'

The smile faded from his face as the dark head inclined forward to look at her, and she had to fight from flinching at the full intensity of those penetrating gold-flecked eyes. 'Whatever nonsense you choose to believe about me,' he told her, 'you must know that it was never my original intention to harm you. Contrary to what you say, I have nothing but the greatest admiration and respect for the small man or woman like yourself who's prepared to work hard in business and make a go of it. If you ever feel inclined to take the time to check it out, I think you'll find Minerva has a pretty healthy track record when it comes to assisting small businesses.'

'You could have fooled me!' The glibness with which he defended his position was nothing less than scandalous. 'Is it supposed to make me feel better knowing I've been picked out for special treatment from you?'

'Not you. Cole.'

'It's the same thing. Remember, he's my partner!' she told him sarcastically.

The lean brown hand, which had been resting casually across his knee, tightened now into a fist. 'You could have got out. You chose not to. If you insist on lying down in the pathway of a moving train, you can't start whimpering when it runs over you.'

'But why should I have to get out of the way?' She met the angry impatience in his eyes with equal uncompromising fury in hers. 'Why should I have to give up my business on some vindictive whim of yours, everything I've slaved for for the past three years? Even if you did offer me a generous price for it! What would you do if someone came along and tried to buy Minerva out? Just hand it over to them with a smile? Of course you wouldn't! You'd fight them no matter what they offered you!' She took a deep breath. 'So why should it be any different for me? Bridge Antiques means just as much to me as Minerva does to you!'

He stood up abruptly and circled the chair that he'd been sitting on, dark and brooding, like some unquiet beast. 'You may not believe this, Jessica, but you sealed your fate the day you teamed up with Cole. Even if I hadn't come along, you'd have ended up losing your business, anyway. He'd have cheated you out of it, one way or another, just like he cheats and steals from everyone. Make no mistake about it, Jessica, he'd have treated you no differently!'

Jessica could feel herself trembling now, as a rage of almost uncontrollable anger welled up inside of her. 'Liar! Filthy liar!' she screeched. Were there no accusations too base for him to fling at Graham?

'Not lies, Jessica. The truth.' He was staring down at her through ominously narrowed eyes. 'Don't try to tell me you don't honestly know what sort of filthy worm Cole really is!'

He had gone too far. She jumped to her feet indignantly, confronting him. 'I'll have you know that my fiancé is a good and decent man, and I love him and will not have you constantly maligning him! If you are determined to strip us of all that we possess—out of some cruel and childish tit-for-tat—I know there isn't much that we can do to defend ourselves. As Graham's already warned me, you're way out of our league. But don't think, Mr Hartt, that just because you've got the whip hand that gives you the right to hurl personal abuse!'

For a moment, he said nothing, just stared at her. 'I really believe you believe what you're saying!' he muttered at last.

She glared at him. 'And I don't give a damn what you believe! You're a low and despicable bully, and I have nothing but contempt for you!'

To her utter astonishment, he reached out and grabbed her by the arm. Then, before she could even attempt to pull away from him, he proceeded to shake her impatiently, as though she were a disobedient pup. 'Good God, Jessica! Is love really that blind?' His grip was a band of steel, digging relentlessly into her flesh. 'Can't you even see what's staring you right in the face?'

He was so close she could smell the sharp, clean smell of him, feel the heat, the power, that exuded from his hard, taut frame. His face was only inches from her own, the wide mouth set in an implacable line, the dark eyes glittering into hers. And an odd sort of panic assailed her, as much a reaction to his physical nearness as it was to the anger in him. 'Let me go!' she yelled, struggling to twist her arm away from him. 'Get your hands off me at once!'

He paid no attention, but instead shook her again. 'Open your eyes, you little fool! What the hell are you thinking of?'

With a gasp of anger, she raised her free hand and took a swing at him with all her strength, feeling a tingle of satisfaction as her palm made resounding contact with the side of his face. 'I told you to let me go!' How dared he try to intimidate her like this!

For a moment that seemed to stretch into eternity, he neither moved nor spoke a word, just stood there, his fingers still locked around her arm, his grey eyes fathomless as they stared into hers. And it was all that Jessica could do to hold that gaze. Some power, some darkness in him, seemed to be drawing her. Closing around her, sapping her will. It frightened her. It was the devil in him, that evil force she had sensed in him from the very start.

A sharp tap on the already opened door suddenly made them both swing round. 'Mr Hartt, there's a young gentleman outside for Miss Langley.' Miss Clutton was hovering in the doorway again, disbelief and disapproval vying for expression on her face.

'Show him in.' He still hadn't moved, but, very slowly now, he loosened his grip on Jessica's arm and let his own arm fall down to his side. A faintly amused smile flickered across his face as Miss Clutton moved out into the hall again. 'Saved by the bell,' was all he said.

A moment later, Graham walked quickly into the room. At the sight of him, Jessica took a hasty step back away from Luke Hartt, all at once uncomfortably conscious of how close she was standing to him, of her own flushed face, of the livid fingermarks, spread like a fan, across the left side of his jaw.

Suspicion flitted visibly across Graham's face as he glanced from one to the other through narrowed eyes, and there was a definite stiffening in his gait as he crossed the room towards them and confronted Hartt. 'What's going on here?' he demanded in a formal voice. 'For what reason was I summoned here?'

Hartt spoke before Jessica had a chance to open her mouth. 'I asked you to come over so you could drive Miss Langley home,' he said, his tone crisp. 'She's had a bit of an accident. I think she's still a little shaken up.'

'An accident? What kind of accident?' Graham turned abruptly to Jessica. 'What the hell's been going on?'

'It's nothing, Graham, really. We were out riding. The horse bolted and I nearly fell. That's all.'

'Out *riding*?' Graham's eyes widened in disbelief. 'What the hell were you out riding for?' Then he added sarcastically, 'I didn't realise you'd come here on a social call.'

Jessica felt a sudden glow of guilt burning her cheeks. Hadn't she known it would look bad? 'I didn't, Graham. You know why I came.' She stepped forward, anxious to placate him. 'It's just that Mr Hartt was going out riding when I arrived, and he said if I wanted to talk to him, I'd have to go along.' She flashed a quick, accusing look at Hartt. It was all his fault—though it wasn't like Graham to act jealous like this.

'How cosy!' Graham straightened stiffly and shot Hartt a quick look of censure before turning his attention back to Jessica. 'And the horse you were riding bolted, you say?'

Jessica nodded. 'There was a shot—a poacher in the woods nearby—and the horse went out of control.'

Graham frowned. 'You realise you could have been killed?'

'I know. In fact, I probably would have been if Mr Hartt hadn't come after me. He saved my life.'

'So it was Luke Hartt to the rescue, was it?' Graham swivelled round with a look of contempt and fixed his gaze on the taller man. 'Not your usual role at all!'

'What's important is that Miss Langley escaped unscathed.' Hartt chose to ignore the gibe. Throughout the entire exchange between Graham and Jessica, he'd remained very still, as though making an effort to control himself. His tone was deliberately flat now as he added, 'However, as I say, she's had a shock. I think you should take her home.'

But Graham seemed determined to press the moral advantage he evidently thought he had. 'I don't know what you were up to when you issued this riding invitation of yours—it sounds very fishy to me—but I want you to know I take serious issue with the way you put my fiancée's life at risk.' He tilted his chin up aggressively. 'I'm afraid it's not enough just to say she escaped unscathed.'

Very slowly, Luke Hartt folded his arms across his chest. 'What are you looking for, Cole?' The lines around his jaw had hardened and a sharp crease deepened between the straight black brows. 'Compensation of some sort?' He smiled a cold and humourless smile. 'That's your style, isn't it? Well, you're out of luck.' The strong, broad shoulders beneath the cashmere sweater seemed to flex. 'On the other hand, if you're looking for a fight...'

'Ah, that's more like it! Throwing your weight around is what you're good at, isn't it, Hartt? But you don't scare me!' Though he took a strategic step back all the same, and added hurriedly, 'And don't worry, compensation's not what's on my mind. I want none of your filthy money, Hartt. I'm just warning you to keep away from Jessica.'

'Let's leave, Graham.' Jessica was all too conscious of the anger she could feel rising in Hartt. And, if things did get out of hand, she knew Graham would be no match for him. She laid one hand protectively on her fiancé's arm. 'Let's leave now. Please.'

He turned towards her. 'OK, my dear.' He took her solicitously by the arm. 'The sooner we get out of here the better. This place stinks!'

Not daring to glance at Hartt, Jessica followed Graham gratefully to the door. She could feel Hartt's temper, like a cauldron, about to boil over at any moment now.

The three of them walked in silence down the corridor towards the front door. Graham first, then Jessica, with Luke Hartt bringing up the rear, his hands thrust deep into his jodhpur pockets, as though he was deliberately restraining them.

Graham paused as he pulled open the big front door and cast a critical eye around the entrance hall, scanning the heavy chandelier, oil paintings on the walls and the pair of life-size marble busts surveying the scene impassively from their twin pedestals. 'Fancy little set-up you've got here, haven't you?' And he shot Hartt a scathing over-the-shoulder glance as he stepped outside. 'Paid for with dirty money, of course. Just like everything you own.'

Anxiety was tightening in Jessica's breast. Graham really ought to drop it now. He was playing with a fire more lethal than he seemed to realise. For the cauldron was bubbling like a volcano now.

She hurried over to the van and climbed quickly into the passenger seat, leaned over and opened the door on the driver's side, as though to tempt Graham more quickly inside. But Graham, unwisely, was taking his time. He lingered in the open doorway of the van and tossed a final gibe at Hartt.

'People like you think they don't have to answer to anyone. Just because you've got plenty of money and friends in high places, you think you bloody own the world. Well, let me tell you...'

It was as though something inside Hartt finally snapped. In a flash, he had stepped forward and banged his fist down hard on the roof of the van, less than a handspan from Graham's face, his body imprisoning the smaller man against the door. 'Look, Cole, you're treading on very dangerous ground. I don't take insults from anybody—and certainly not from trash like you! If I've refrained so far from knocking your teeth down your throat, it's for one reason only. Miss Langley has already had one upset this morning, and I don't think she should be subjected to another one. But I warn you, don't push me too far!'

Graham's face had turned very white. His back was pressed against the door. 'Lay one hand on me,' he stuttered, 'and I'll report you for assault!'

Hartt leaned over him with a threatening smile. 'You know, you're very clever, Cole. Coming here and putting on that jealous boyfriend act. Hoping to take the heat off yourself. But you don't fool me—though I find it easier now to believe all the stories I've heard. You're a real con-man, aren't you? You never miss a trick.' He paused and raked the pale face with flint-hard eyes. 'But I'll tell you something. Neither do I. And, just in case you haven't got the message yet, I'll tell you something else. Your con-man days are over. I'm going to destroy you, Cole.' His lips curled menacingly as he went on, 'I'm going to trample all over you. And, when I've finished doing that, I'm going to grind the verminous pieces into the ground and bury them so deep they'll never see daylight or breathe air

again. You may not be fully convinced of it yet,
but your crimes have finally caught up with you.
I'm on to you, Cole. And I intend to put a stop to
you!'

He stepped back abruptly and gestured to
Graham to get in the van—which he did, with no
hesitation at all—then slammed the door shut after
him. 'Now get the hell out of here and don't let me
see your face again!'

As Graham started the engine with a trembling
hand, Jessica reached out to touch him sympathetically on the arm. Luke Hartt was a bastard, a con-
scienceless, bullying bastard to threaten him like
that. And she hated him for it.

With a crash of gears, the van jerked forwards
and Jessica turned to steal one final swift glance at
the tall, dark figure standing in the driveway, head
high, hands on hips, triumphantly watching their
retreat. And again she felt the dark force that was
in him reaching out to her, and hastily snatched her
eyes away. She shivered, breathed in deeply and
closed her eyes. But she could not shake off the icy
presentiment that gripped her soul.

For suddenly she knew beyond a doubt that her
whole safe little world was about to come crashing
down about her ears.

CHAPTER FOUR

THE disaster that was to follow, however, did not come immediately. Instead, there ensued a puzzling and unexpected lull—and a series of weird happenings that left Jessica feeling totally bewildered and confused.

The first sign that something strange was afoot was the sudden, abrupt closure of Spinning Wheel Antiques. One day, it was soaking up all the local trade as usual, the next, the door was padlocked and the blinds pulled down. Jessica surveyed this latest development with mingled suspicion and surprise. What the devil was Hartt up to now?

'Just be grateful for small mercies,' Deirdre advised her when Jessica expressed her disbelief. 'It looks like he's decided to let you off the hook.'

It seemed unlikely, somehow. Especially in the light of that nasty scene with Graham at the Old Mill House. Hartt had hardly given the impression then of a man poised to dispense clemency. Yet all the evidence seemed to point that way. Suddenly, Jessica's and Graham's visits to the auction rooms were no longer bedevilled by the presence of Miss Clutton, or some other of Hartt's minions, all too predictably outbidding them. On the surface, at least, things were returning to normal again.

Jessica hadn't laid eyes on Hartt again since the day of the riding accident. He was up in London, according to local reports. Nor had she had any form of contact with him—though, in a gesture that was as bizarre as it was inexplicable, he had phoned Bridge Antiques a couple of days afterwards, while both Graham and Jessica were out, and spoken briefly to Deirdre.

'What exactly did he say?' Jessica was both puzzled and curious. Was this a new twist to the game?

The blonde-haired woman shook her head. 'He didn't say much at all, as a matter of fact. Just asked how you were—if you'd recovered from the accident. I told him you were fine and asked if he wanted to leave a message. He said he didn't—and hung up.'

It made no sense. 'You're absolutely certain it was him?'

'Oh, yes,' Deirdre assured her. 'He said who he was.' And her round face creased into a thoughtful smile. 'But I think I would have known it was him, anyway. Not many men have such a distinctive voice.'

No, thought Jessica sceptically. Nor such a distinctive manner of settling old grudges, either, come to that.

But, about a week later, she began seriously to wonder if maybe Deirdre had been right. Perhaps Hartt really had abandoned his campaign at last. For, one afternoon, quite out of the blue, a man whom she had never seen before walked into the shop and bought the infamous *secrétaire* for six thousand pounds, cash. And she was instinctively certain that the stranger had been sent by Hartt—indicating that he did have a thin streak of decency in him, after all. Or, at least, was capable of a change of heart.

Graham, for his part, however, was not convinced. 'He's up to something. I know he is,' he kept insisting, with an air of certainty that seemed to grow with the evidence to the contrary. 'You heard how he threatened me. I tell you, he's not the type to suddenly go soft.'

That much was undoubtedly true. 'Maybe he thought he'd done enough. Maybe he just got bored with the whole thing.'

'Don't believe it!' Graham scoffed the suggestion aside. 'You don't know the man. When he starts something, he sticks with it to the bitter end. And he's out to get me. You were there when he said it, Jessica. Don't tell me you've forgotten that!'

'Of course not.' How could she ever forget what had passed that day? Hartt's fury, the terrible things he had said to Graham and, somehow most disturbing of all, the deep sense of uneasiness he had stirred in her. Almost guiltily now, she thrust that memory aside and tried to talk Graham round. 'Look, he's probably just come to his senses, that's all. He's finally realised that what he was doing was way out of proportion to the supposed crime.' She smiled reassuringly into Graham's anxious face and reached out to lay one hand affectionately over his. 'You can see for yourself that he's given up.' And she nodded to the business accounts book they'd been working on. 'We're actually in the black again.'

'That doesn't mean a thing!' Impatiently, Graham snatched his hand away. 'The only reason he's backed off is to lull us into a false sense of security. I'm surprised you're not capable of working that out for yourself.' His eyes narrowed accusingly. 'What did he say to you that day to influence you? I know that something was going on when I arrived.'

'You're wrong!' Why did he keep returning again and again these days to this misguided theme of jealousy? It only upset her. 'The only reason I'm saying he's dropped that ridiculous vendetta of his is because of all the evidence.' She leaned towards him, anxious to set his mind at rest. She hated to see him so edgy and worried all time. He was normally so cool, so calm, but that confrontation with Hartt had badly frightened him. 'Can't you see for yourself that he's finally lost interest in us?'

'No, I'm afraid I can't!' Abruptly, he got to his feet and started to pace the floor. 'All I can see is that he's probably, right this minute, plotting something far more sinister behind the scenes.' He flung an angry look at her. 'I've always said it, Jessica. That man is dangerous.'

Jessica dropped her eyes. 'What could he do?' Though he was really only echoing the same secret fear she'd always had.

'Anything! He could do anything!' He whirled round to confront her now. 'Believe me, I'm serious.' And, seeing the sudden look of doubt in her face, he crossed back to the desk where she was sitting and leaned towards her urgently. 'Jessica, we've got to get out of here. Sell up. The shop, the flat, the whole damned lot, and make a fresh start somewhere else. As far away as we can get. Out of the reach of that bastard Hartt.'

Slowly, Jessica shook her head, remembering how Hartt had once warned her against such a move. If it was true that right now he was only biding his time, it would be pointless to run. 'It wouldn't work,' she told Graham now. 'He'd only come after us.'

'We could try.' Graham's tone was earnest, almost pleading. He reached for her hand. 'We could change our identities. Play all sorts of tricks on him. If we were really smart, he'd never manage to track us down.'

But Jessica could not agree. 'Right now, we still don't know if we've got anything to be worried about. Maybe he's not plotting anything.' She appealed to him. 'Let's not do anything rash just yet.'

Angrily, he straightened. 'What has to happen before you're convinced? Do I have to be found lying face-down in a ditch somewhere?' He was trembling. 'For that's what could happen—whether you choose to believe it or not!'

His words sent a cold chill, like icy fingers, prickling across Jessica's scalp. She stared at him. 'Graham, that's preposterous!'

'Is it?' Stiff-legged with exasperation, he swung away, heading for the door, then paused for a moment to deliver his parting shot. 'You're going to regret this, Jessica. When it's too late, you're going to be sorry you didn't listen to me!' Then he was gone, slamming the door behind him, and Jessica was left alone, staring disconsolately after him.

He was exaggerating, of course, she hurriedly reassured herself. Hartt was a ruthless, unforgiving man, but surely he wasn't a criminal? It was just that Graham was upset. He was letting his imagination run away with him.

There was no arguing with him, though. Over the next week or so, he relentlessly kept the pressure up, inciting her with increasing urgency to sell up and move to another area. And, as the inevitable tension between the two of them began to mount, it took all of Jessica's willpower and self-control to stand by the decision she'd made. It was for Graham's good as well as her own, she kept telling herself. And he'd realise that eventually.

But then it happened. The following Friday evening, Graham failed to return from a buying trip. He'd left early that morning for Oxford, and Jessica had expected him back well before closing time. But, as she and Deirdre locked up for the night, there was still no sign of him.

'I wouldn't worry if I were you,' Deirdre told her kindly, seeing the concern in her boss's eye. 'He's probably just got held up.'

Jessica nodded. 'Probably.' Though she had a feeling, deep in her bones, that the explanation was not as simple as that. And, next morning, when Graham still failed to show and a phone call to his landlady confirmed that he hadn't returned the previous night, she was even more certain that she had genuine cause to be alarmed.

Deirdre continued to be sceptical. 'I'm sure nothing's happened to him,' she assured her friend over mid-morning coffee. 'After all, it's not the first time he's stayed away overnight.'

'I know.' Though Jessica never did it herself, it wasn't unusual for Graham to sleep over at a hotel when he went to a sale outside the immediate vicinity. 'But he always telephones to let me know.' She sighed and ran her fingers tiredly through her chestnut hair. 'He knows I worry. And especially now. He wouldn't just spend the night somewhere and not let me know.' And she pursed her lips and stared unseeingly into her coffee-cup. 'You know, Deirdre, I've horrible suspicion our friend Luke Hartt has got something to do with this.'

'Like what?'

'I don't know, but he's out to get Graham. I told you that.'

Deirdre stared back at her through doubtful eyes. 'You're not suggesting Luke Hartt's kidnapped him or something, are you?'

'Maybe something even worse.'

'That's a crazy idea!' Deirdre shook her sensible blonde head dismissively. 'Hartt wouldn't do a thing like that.'

Wasn't that what Jessica had once thought, too? And hadn't she scoffed at Graham's warnings, just as Deirdre was scoffing at her now? 'I'm not so sure,' she worriedly told the older girl. 'Graham warned me something like this might happen. He was really scared, you know. And I didn't listen to him.' She bit guiltily at her lower lip. 'If anything's happened to him, it's all my fault.' That's what Graham had warned her, and it was true.

'Don't be silly.' Deirdre leaned across and laid a comforting hand upon her arm. 'Nothing's happened to him, Jessica. Believe me, Graham's perfectly capable of looking after himself. You'll hear from him soon enough. Just wait and see.'

But the day went by and still there was no word from him. In a state of near-desperation, Jessica spent the evening phoning round every hospital between Oxford and Harbingdon, and when that—mercifully—drew a blank, she finally forced herself to do what she'd been putting off doing all along and reported him missing to the police.

Yet something told her that was not enough. The solution to the mystery, she was certain, lay in other hands. Luke Hartt's. And when, the following evening, on returning from an errand in the village, Deirdre informed her casually, 'I hear Luke Hartt's back in residence at the Old Mill House,' she knew precisely what she had to do.

This time, alongside the Porsche, a large Mercedes and an even larger Cadillac were parked. It looked like Hartt had company. Well, that was just too bad, Jessica decided, stepping out of the old, white-painted van and striding resolutely up to the big front door. He'd just have to tear himself away from his visitors for a while. There was no way she would leave here without seeing him.

A pretty, young, uniformed maid opened the door. 'Good evening, madam.' There was a note of polite enquiry in her voice.

'I've come to see Mr Hartt.'

The girl regarded her unlikely garb—a simple summer skirt and top. 'Are you one of the dinner guests?' she enquired, quite clearly not believing for one second that she was.

'No. I've come to see Mr Hartt on private, and urgent, business.'

'Then you'd better come in.'

'Thank you.' At least, this time, she wasn't going to have to battle her way into the house.

'And what name is it, please?'

'Jessica Langley.'

'If you'll just wait here for a moment, Miss Langley, I'll go and tell Mr Hartt you're here.'

How very civilised, Jessica reflected as the girl disappeared down a corridor at the far end of the hall. Not the sort of welcome she'd been anticipating at all. Though the real welcome—or lack of it!— would come, of course, from Hartt himself. She glanced nervously around her, feeling the pale, cold eyes of the two marble busts regarding her imperiously from their pedestals. Hartt would be furious, of course. He would very probably make a scene, threaten to eject her forcibly. Well, she would just have to stand her ground and force him to confess what he'd done with Graham.

'Follow me, please.' Jessica jumped as the maid reappeared soundlessly at her side. 'Mr Hartt will see you now.'

So he had consented to honour her with a few crumbs of his precious time! That was a start. Relieved and apprehensive at the same time, she followed the girl's neat back through an eighteenth-century geometry of corridors, till they reached a panelled door at the back of the house.

The door was opened. 'In here, Miss Langley. Please go ahead.'

She'd expected to be shown into some small ante-room where Hartt would be waiting for her on his own. Instead, her eyes widened with surprise as she found herself stepping into a large and exquisitely decorated dining-room, where six elegant people were seated round a candlelit, white damask-covered dining-table, agleam with silver and crystal and porcelain. And she stifled a gasp of mingled confusion and dismay as the tinkle of laughter and conversation around the table abruptly died, and six pairs of eyes turned curiously to look at her.

'Why, Jessica, don't hang back. Come in and make yourself at home.' He had risen to his feet at the head of the table, a tall, imposing figure in an immaculate black dinner-suit. And he was smiling at her, a deliberately provocative smile. He glanced round at the three women and two men who were following the scene with interest now. 'This is Miss Langley, a neighbour of mine.' And the smile curled with wicked pleasure around the corners of the fine, wide mouth. 'So, Jessica, what can I do for you?'

Jessica stared with angry resentment at him. He obviously found it amusing to make her look foolish in front of his guests. 'I need to have a word with you,' she told him in a clear, tight voice. Then added with steely emphasis, 'In private, if you don't mind.'

He gave a shrug of mock-regret and raised one coal-black eyebrow at her. 'I'm afraid you've chosen a rather inopportune moment,' he said. 'As you can see, I'm otherwise engaged.' In the flickering candlelight, the lines of the strong, bronzed face were at once intensified and enhanced, the penetrating grey eyes, behind their surface amusement, deep and mysterious, and the dark hair as smooth and glossy as a raven's wing. If only he was not so devilishly handsome, Jessica found herself thinking with regret, he'd be so much easier to hate.

Impatiently, she pushed the thought away, forcibly reminding herself of the villainous bully that lay beneath, and straightened her shoulders aggressively. 'All I'm asking is a couple of minutes of your time. It's important.'

'Not that important, surely, Jessica? You wouldn't expect me to abandon my guests?' He tossed her a taunting smile. 'We can talk later, if you insist. In the mean time, why don't you join us for dinner?' As he snapped his fingers, a couple of waiters appeared from nowhere and proceeded to lay an additional place, on Hartt's right, between a beautiful dark-haired girl in a blood-red evening dress and a slightly portly fair-haired man who appeared as bemused by the entire spectacle as Jessica herself.

'I'd rather just have a quick word with you now,' she insisted lamely, already knowing it was a waste of time.

'I'm afraid not, Jessica.' Very pointedly, he re-seated himself. 'We can talk later, when my guests have gone.' And he waved his wine glass at the silk-upholstered dining-chair that was already waiting in position for her. 'Please sit. I think we've held up the proceedings long enough.'

Jessica hovered uncomfortably, uncertain what her next move should be. Should she turn and walk out with her tail between her legs, defeated yet again by this loathsome man? Or should she stay and subject herself to what would undoubtedly turn out to be an excruciating couple of hours—with at least the prospect of being able to complete her mission eventually?

With a false smile, she stepped forward into the room. She would play his game—since that appeared to be the only way of getting anywhere.

'How very kind.' And, self-consciously but with her head held high, she strode defiantly across the room and seated herself next to the girl in red. 'What an unexpected pleasure,' she beamed.

It was only then that she recognised the figure seated at the opposite end of the table to Hartt: Miss Clutton, this evening looking severe but distinguished in a grey silk dress. She was the only one who failed to smile now, as Hartt quickly introduced Jessica to the other guests. In fact, if looks could kill, Jessica would have fallen to the floor as lifeless as the chunk of veal that was being shovelled by the waiter on to her plate. But at least the other guests showed no hostility. Quite the opposite, in fact.

They were not the types that Jessica would have expected to find gathered round Luke Hartt's dinner table. Fiona and Louis Baxby—she a pretty, red-haired psychoanalyst, he a consultant economist working for the Treasury, a man with a quick wit and a dry sense of humour, a perfect foil for the caring, insightful sensitivity of his wife. He gallantly helped the newcomer to a glass of Château Lafite. 'I never guessed I'd be lucky enough to have two lovely ladies sitting next to me this evening,' he smiled.

Then there was Annette Chantel—the girl in the red dress sitting on Jessica's left—and her charming husband Gérard, the two of them recently returned from a diplomatic tour in the Middle East where Gérard had risen to First Commercial Secretary at the French Embassy. They were, all four, a far cry from the vain, fluff-headed company Jessica had somehow supposed Luke Hartt would keep. And she found the revelation mildly disquieting. It seemed the more she discovered about the man, the more of an enigma he became. Perhaps she would never manage to pin him down.

The red-haired Fiona, the gold of her dress softly complimenting the discreet pallor of her skin, was leaning interestedly towards her now. 'Have you always lived in this part of the world?' she asked.

'No.' Jessica was already starting to relax. 'As a matter of fact, I only moved here about three years ago. But I like it so much that nothing could induce me to leave now.'

She glanced significantly across at Hartt as Fiona answered, 'I don't know the area well, of course, but, from what I've seen, I find your feelings perfectly understandable.'

The gold-flecked eyes narrowed critically as he lost no time in cutting in. 'Understandable, perhaps—but foolish nevertheless. One should always allow for the possibility of changing circumstances. In this world, Jessica, I'm afraid, change in all things is inevitable.'

She flicked a challenge at him. 'Though, where it is unjustly imposed, it should be resisted, don't you think?'

He shrugged broad shoulders. 'Maybe, if you believe in struggle for struggle's sake. Sometimes it may be pointless, even self-defeating, to resist. Quite often, it is in the individual's best interests simply to bend to the inevitable.'

'How very oriental!' Annette laughed. 'I think, Luke, you must have been an Arab in a former life. That is exactly their philosophy.'

Hartt drained his glass. 'Quite possible,' he answered with an inscrutable smile. 'I'm sure that I've been many different things in many different lives.'

The Frenchman shook his head and smiled. 'Aha! We have a split personality by the sound of things!'

'Not split, just highly complex,' Fiona corrected him. 'And, if you ever were an Arab, Luke,' she went on with a mischievous wink, 'I doubt very much that you were such a passive, fatalistic one. A wild and warlike Berber would be more your style!'

So at least she and the psychoanalyst were agreed on one thing, Jessica thought ruefully. Luke Hartt was a troublemaker to his fingertips!

As it turned out—and much to Jessica's surprise—the evening was far from excruciating. In fact, had it not been for the emotionally disruptive presence of Hartt, constantly reminding her of the reason for her being there, it would have ranked as one of the most enjoyable evenings that Jessica had passed for a very long time. The conversation was stimulating and full of good humour, the food exquisite and the wine flowed abundantly. By the time that coffee and liqueurs were being served, she felt relaxed and mellow, her troubles relegated to the background for a change.

'It's been so nice meeting you,' Annette told her as she stirred her coffee with a silver spoon. 'If you're in France at all this summer, you must come and visit us. We'll be spending as much time as we possibly can at our place in Cannes before Gérard's next posting overseas.' She turned her dark head to Jessica with a smile. 'Luke will give you our address. We're near neighbours of the Judge and his wife, you know.'

Jessica frowned, uncomprehending.

'Luke's parents,' Annette explained. 'When Judge Hartt retired a couple of years ago, they moved to the south of France. Luke's mother's French, you see.' She laughed. 'You must surely have detected the wild Gallic spirit in him!'

Perhaps, though that was not exactly how she had defined it herself. And, as Annette turned away to ask Luke—'And when are you coming across the Channel to visit your spiritual home?'—the falseness of her own position suddenly came home to Jessica. Her status had been grievously misinterpreted by the present company. They thought she was a friend of Luke's. And nothing could be farther from the truth.

As Hartt nodded mock-deferentially towards Miss Clutton, the *éminence grise* at the opposite end of the table and answered, 'That all depends on when my secretary will allow me some time off,' Jessica felt suddenly brought up short by the reminder that for the past few hours she'd allowed the wine and the elegant civility of her surroundings to go completely to her head. How could she have forgotten, even for one moment, who this man was? He was no less than her mortal enemy, a man who took sadistic pleasure in playing deadly little games with other people's lives.

Shortly afterwards, the party broke up and it was with genuine regret that Jessica bade the two couples goodbye. It was a little sad to think that their paths and hers would probably never cross again. But, if there was one thing she had learned tonight, it was that there was no truth whatsoever in the axiom that you can judge a man by his friends.

She glanced at her watch as she waited in the drawing-room while Luke went outside to see off his guests. It was just after one o'clock. The brief encounter she had planned had somehow stretched into four whole hours. Miss Clutton was sitting in an armchair close by, eyeing her with a hostility that had never diminished throughout the entire evening. 'I'd no idea it was so late,' Jessica offered woodenly, really just for something to say.

The woman's thin lips tightened and a pair of disapproving eyes peered out through the lenses of the steel-rimmed spectacles. 'Yes, it is rather,' she answered in clipped tones. 'Oughtn't you to be getting home?'

A flash of anger flared in response to the blatant reprimand. Miss Clutton evidently thought that Jessica had no right to be there at all. 'I'll be leaving just as soon as I've spoken to Mr Hartt—if that's any concern of yours.' Simple civility aside, the woman was definitely out of line.

But Miss Clutton was not so easily put off her stride. 'I don't know what you think you're going to gain by coming here, but I would advise you to leave Mr Hartt alone. He doesn't need types like you sniffing around, trying to ingratiate themselves. Why don't you just go back where you came from? You're not wanted here.'

'Now you just hang on!' Jessica jerked forward furiously in her seat. Who did the old witch think she was, talking to her like that? 'It seems to me you're ever so slightly overstepping your authority. It's hardly for you to say whether I'm welcome here or not.'

'Oh, but it is. It's part of my job to protect Mr Hartt from the likes of you.' The thin lips curled disapprovingly. 'You see, I know what your game is, Miss Langley. I've met your type before.'

'Have you? And what type is that?!'

'The usual type.' Miss Clutton gave a knowing, dismissive laugh. 'I suppose it's only to be expected, of course. My employer is both extremely wealthy and capable of pulling a great many strings. You'll always find a certain type of female eager to trade favours with such a man.'

Jessica could have hit her. 'Why, you——!' She caught her breath. 'Let me put you right about that! I——'

'Excuse me, ladies. Am I interrupting something?' Hartt was standing in the drawing-room doorway, watching them, a look of amused superiority playing around his lips.

'Not at all. Miss Langley and I were simply having a little chat.' The words dropped like steel hooks from her lips as, with a final look of warning at Jessica, Miss Clutton rose slowly from her chair. 'I'm off to bed now. Good night, Mr Hartt.'

'Good night, Miss Clutton.' He stood aside politely to let her pass, as, like a chill wind, she stalked past him and out the door.

He closed the door behind her and came across the thick-pile carpet with unhurried strides, stopping just a few feet away from Jessica. 'I see you've been upsetting my secretary again.'

Jessica folded her arms defensively across her chest. He was so close, his gaze so disturbing, and she hated having to look up at him. 'Unfortunately, Miss Clutton appears to have got rather the wrong idea about me.'

He raised a curious eyebrow at her as he sat down in the chair Miss Clutton had vacated just a moment before. 'Oh, and what idea has she got?'

'She seems to think I've got designs on you. She obviously believes I've come here to throw my body at you in an effort to extract some favour in exchange.'

The grey eyes travelled slowly over her as he leaned back in his chair. 'And that, you're trying to tell me, is not the case?'

Jessica felt indignant colour rush to her face 'It most certainly is not!' How dared he even suggest such a thing!

'Pity.' He stretched his long legs out in front of him. 'That would have spiced things up considerably.' Then he paused deliberately and smiled. 'I thought perhaps you'd missed me, dearest Jessica.'

'Missed you! Like a hole in the head!'

He continued to smile. 'So I take it you noticed my withdrawal from your affairs?'

'I noticed. Though I'm also aware it was only for show. A cover for something else.'

He shook his head. 'What a suspicious mind you have.' And gazed levelly across at her. 'So, tell me, why *are* you here, if not to barter your beautiful body in exchange for my good offices?'

Again she felt the colour heighten in her cheeks as she answered, her tone clipped, 'I think you

know perfectly well why I'm here. Graham, my
fiancé, has disappeared.'

He raked her face with a malicious eye. 'I would
have thought that a cause for celebration. But I can
see from your demeanour that you unwisely judge
it otherwise. Don't tell me you've come here looking
for my sympathy?'

'I've come here looking for explanations, Mr
Hartt.' She met the mocking grey gaze with green
ice. 'I think you know what's happened to him,
and I demand that you tell me and that you release
him immediately—unharmed.'

'I very much regret to say, dear Jessica, that I
can't do that.'

'What do you mean?' Jessica felt a sudden tightening in her breast at the implication of his words.

Hartt shook his dark head at her and smiled a
dry and humourless smile. 'I can't do it, simply
because it is neither within my power to tell you
what has happened to the man nor to return him
to you, unharmed or otherwise.' He frowned.
'Whatever made you think I had anything to do
with his disappearance, anyway?'

'I know you're behind it. I'm sure of it.'

He laced his long fingers together and rested his
chin against his thumbs. 'Poor Jessica,' he said.
'So he's gone and left you in the lurch? Well, if
you cast your mind back, you'll recall it's no more
than I warned you he would do.'

She might have known he'd try and change the
situation round on her! Use it to cast another unfair
slur on Graham's character! But she was wise to
his tricks by now. 'Don't try that sort of line with
me, Mr Hartt. Graham hasn't left me in the lurch.

Something's happened to him. And I'm absolutely certain you know what that something is.'

'Of course I know!' He flung her a look of total contempt. 'What's happened to him is that, as I could have predicted long ago, he's got cold feet and taken off. I'm only surprised that you're not capable of reaching that conclusion for yourself. But then, as I remember pointing out to you already once before, for a clearly intelligent young woman you're remarkably inept at seeing what's staring you in the face. When it comes to matters of the heart, at any rate.' He flicked at some imaginary speck of dust on the sleeve of his immaculate black dinner-jacket. 'Forgive me for asking, but have you checked your bank account, by any chance?'

What was he suggesting now? 'And why on earth should I do that?'

The steel-grey gaze locked into hers. 'How long has Cole been gone?'

'Since Friday—as if you didn't know!'

'And this is Sunday—or the early hours of Monday now.' The dark eyes continued to hold hers relentlessly. 'As soon as the banks open, later today, I suggest that you check the state of your business account. I think you'll find that whatever funds you had in it have unaccountably disappeared.'

'That's a vile suggestion!'

'I admit at times the truth can be hard to take.'

'The truth! And what would you know about the truth?! Lies and character assassination—that's all you know!' She was trembling with outrage at the enormity of what he'd said. Didn't he have any scruples at all? Didn't it matter to him that he was slandering an innocent man?

He shrugged. 'Believe what you like. I'm not going to make a scene. After all, it makes no difference to me whether I'm right or not—and you will have ample opportunity to find out one way or the other for yourself.' He shifted forward in his seat. 'And now, if you don't mind, I think I'll call it a day.'

'Not quite so fast! You haven't told me where Graham is!'

'Sorry, Jessica. Not tonight.' He glanced at the slim gold watch at his wrist, then laid his hands, palms downward, along the arms of the chair and, very deliberately, stood up. 'I think you ought to spend the night here. I noticed it's pretty foggy out there.'

She didn't even hear the last part of his speech. After the first few words, she'd more or less stopped listening. 'What do you mean "Not tonight"? So you do know, after all!' She leapt to her feet accusingly. 'Tell me! Where is he? What have you done with him?'

A strange look flitted across his face, as though he regretted revealing so much. 'I haven't done anything with him, Jessica. That much I ask you to believe.' He straightened and ran one hand across his hair as he added, 'But I think I might just know where he is.'

'Tell me!' she demanded.

But he shook his head. 'I already told you, not tonight.' An expression of total intractability settled across his features now. 'Don't argue. We'll discuss it in the morning, and not before.'

'I want to discuss it now!' She followed him as he started to move away. 'I think I have a right to be told. I insist that you tell me right away!'

He ignored her. 'I'll show you to your room now if that's OK.'

'It's *not* OK.' She was right behind him, one hand reaching out insistently to touch his arm. 'I want you to tell me this minute where Graham is.'

He shook her off as though she were a fly. 'You can have the room next to Miss Clutton. I think you should be comfortable.'

'Damn you! Won't you listen to me?' In total frustration, she grabbed at his sleeve, struggling with all her puny strength to force him to turn round and look at her. 'Tell me where he is!'

He swung round then, catching her totally off guard, and grabbed her by the arm. 'You listen to me, young lady! I've had just about enough of your antics!' His fingers pressed against her skin, as cool and inescapable as an iron band. 'There's one thing you should learn about me and learn fast. When I say something, I generally mean it. And I have absolutely no patience with people who keep arguing all the time.'

'Is that a fact! Well, maybe it wouldn't be a bad thing if you started getting used to it for a change!' Anger and defiance flashed from her eyes. 'You're far too used to having things your own damned way. You think you can get away with anything. Well, I'm not going to let you. I think it's high time that somebody stood up to you for a change!'

'Really? Is that what you think?' To her surprise, he smiled.

She blinked and tried to move away from him. 'That's what I think,' she spat.

But in one deft movement he had pulled her close to him, so that her body was suddenly pressed against the lean, hard strength of his. 'And tell me, Jessica, what do you think of this?' Then his arm slid round her back, pinning her to his chest, and, before she could snatch her head away, his mouth had descended on hers, claiming her lips in a startling and fiercely compelling kiss.

Jessica could not think at all. Reason, logic—all these things—in the instant that his lips met hers, were swept away. There was no room, amid the sensuous explosion that ripped through her, for rationality or calculation of any kind. All she knew was that her flesh was suddenly burning, responding helplessly—almost willingly, it seemed—to the fire in his.

Gently, but insistently, he was prising her lips apart, his mouth moving possessively over hers, awakening in her a hunger she had never known before. And she gasped and stiffened in his arms as she felt his tongue slide deliciously between her teeth, teasing, exploring the secret inner softness of her mouth. She shuddered as his free hand moved round to cover her breast, the fingers circling tantalisingly around its sensitive, thrusting peak.

She seemed to hang suspended in time, a puppet, a plaything in his arms, her will somehow sapped by the deep, dark power in him that was closing all around her, filling her entire being, dragging her down.

'No!' Belatedly, Jessica pulled away, trembling, her breath rasping roughly in her throat as she staggered clumsily away from him. 'Stop it!'

The gold-flecked eyes were staring down into hers, hypnotic, dark and strangely menacing. But she felt his hand drop abruptly from her waist, releasing her, and with a stifled cry, almost of pain, she took another step away from him.

He didn't move, just stood there staring down at her. And, when he spoke at last, his voice seemed to come from far away. 'I think I'd better show you to your room,' he said.

Her heart was still fluttering dementedly inside her breast. 'I can't possibly sleep here!' The very idea was unthinkable.

'I'm afraid you'll have to. I've no intention of allowing you to drive home alone in that fog.'

'I can manage.' Suddenly just the thought of being with him in this house was frightening. 'Really I can,' she tried to insist.

'No, you can't. And even if you can, we both know how unreliable that van of yours can be. I'm not going to let you risk getting stranded at this time of night.' He stepped back and let his hands drop to his sides. 'Don't worry,' he told her with a faintly self-mocking smile. 'You'll be perfectly safe. I won't be coming to beat your door down in the middle of the night.'

Jessica stared down at the carpet in sudden embarrassment. Then flicked her eyes up to meet his again. 'I'll stay, if you promise that you'll tell me where Graham is.'

He started to move towards the door. 'I'll explain everything in the morning, I promise you.'

She followed him upstairs, suddenly weary, longing for sleep. And, as he bade her a brief goodnight, she stepped inside the bedroom gratefully and closed the door. Tomorrow, she would be relieved of the suspense of wondering what had become of Graham. Hartt would keep his promise. She was sure of that.

But, as she slid between the cool, soft sheets, she was aware of a new threat hanging over her. And she closed her eyes and tried to chase from her mind the burning memory of that kiss. And of how, for an instant, the man who was her mortal enemy had seemed to touch her very soul.

Just the thought that it was so struck a new kind of terror in her heart.

CHAPTER FIVE

JESSICA awoke with a start next morning, surprised to discover that she had slept at all. An early-August sun was pouring in through rose-peach curtains, suffusing the room in a warm, golden light, and she could hear the sound of voices floating up to her from the garden below. Yawning, she leaned across to the bedside table and looked at her watch. Then sat up with a start when she saw that it was nearly half-past eight. She had planned to be up and gone long before now!

It took her less than twenty minutes to shower, dress and run a comb quickly through her chestnut hair. She had no make-up with her, not even a lipstick—she'd scarcely been expecting to stay overnight!—but her clear, pale complexion had no real need of it. Besides, her appearance was really the last thing on Jessica's mind. Right now, her two principal concerns were, firstly, to extract details of Graham's whereabouts from Hartt—then to put as much space as quickly as possible between herself and the Old Mill House.

It being a Monday, and assuming that he normally returned to London after the weekend, she was half afraid that Hartt might have already left. But on the directions of a grey-haired woman armed with brushes and brooms whom she almost literally bumped into half-way down the stairs, she found him taking breakfast in the breakfast-room.

He was wearing a navy silk robe, a pair of matching silk-tasselled slippers on his feet, and a copy of *The Financial Times* was spread out on the table in front of him. He glanced up instantly as she walked in. 'Good morning,' he greeted her, smiling. 'Just in time to join me for breakfast. Did you sleep well?'

'Yes, thank you.' She sat down awkwardly, acutely aware of the scanty manner in which he was clad. The robe reached only to his knees, and as he folded the newspaper and laid it to one side she couldn't help surmising that, very probably, he was naked underneath.

Perhaps he could read her mind, for he told her, 'I hope you don't object to my attire? I think that dressing before breakfast is highly uncivilised.' His dark hair was still wet from the shower, lending him an improbably appealing look. The grey eyes smiled across at her. 'Probably some irrational legacy from my rebellious adolescence—after a childhood of always being required to appear at table fully dressed. These days, I'm afraid, my house guests just have to put up with me.'

Jessica reached for a tall jug of freshly squeezed orange juice and poured herself a glass. 'It doesn't bother me,' she said. But she deliberately kept her eyes averted all the same. For some reason, it was quite impossible to look at him and not remember the way it had felt to be held in his arms last night, the way his lips had scorched against hers, the intimate touch of his hand on her breast. And to burn with shame at the memory of it. For one mad, extraordinary moment, he had seemed to turn her inside-out.

Her tone was clipped as she went on, 'I've no doubt you're in as much of a hurry to get started with the day as I am, Mr Hartt. Perhaps we could get down to business right away?' And she flicked up her eyes impatiently to lock with his. 'You promised to tell me where Graham is.'

Hartt leaned back his head and looked at her through lowered lids. 'All in good time, Jessica. All in good time. As it happens, I'm not in any hurry at all.' He gestured at the dishes of sausage and bacon and eggs, the bowls of mueslis and assorted cereals, the plates of fresh rolls and croissants and toast that were spread in generous abundance over the linen tablecloth. 'Let's eat first and deal with such distasteful matters afterwards. I believe in starting the day off on a pleasant note.'

Evidently! thought Jessica. And equally evidently he intended conducting the proceedings precisely in accordance with his own desires. She should have expected that. With an ungracious toss of her head, she snatched up a slice of toast and dropped it on to her plate. 'I'm not hungry,' she informed him before he could say anything. It happened to be far from true, but she had no desire to accept any further hospitality from him. Besides, he wasn't the only one with a rebellious streak.

'Suit yourself.' He helped himself unconcernedly to bacon and sausage and scrambled egg, and poured strong black coffee from a silver pot. 'Personally, I believe in having a substantial breakfast. It's the one meal of the day I invariably take my time about.'

Jessica glared furiously at her plate. Why couldn't he just tell her what she wanted to know and be done with it? Why did he insist on detaining her here against her will, making conversation, amusing himself with her discomfiture as usual? But she knew better than to waste time arguing by now. That would only anger him. And, at least, this morning he seemed in a fairly peaceable frame of mind.

She helped herself to a spoonful of golden honey from a comb. 'Isn't Miss Clutton joining us?' she asked, noticing that the table was only set for two.

'Miss Clutton had breakfast hours ago. She's probably back at her desk in London by now.'

Thank heaven for that! Jessica bit into her toast. 'I can see that you make her earn that handsome salary of hers.'

'Of course.' He eyed her with amusement now. 'Not that Miss Clutton has ever needed to be pushed into doing any of the little jobs I've asked of her. She's always most willing.'

Jessica sniffed. 'How very characteristic that, out of all the tens of thousands of ordinary, decent ones available, you managed to find yourself a secretary as totally unethical as yourself.'

He shook his head. 'Don't be so hard on her. She's not that bad.'

He was laughing at her again. Jessica straightened defensively in her chair. 'I suppose you find such blind devotion flattering. No doubt you encourage her to act as though she was personally responsible for your well-being.'

The dark eyes twinkled. 'It's part of her job to try to guard my privacy. Though, I admit, she can be a little over-zealous at times.'

'A little!' Jessica cast disparaging green eyes at him, striving not to notice the sun-bronzed darkness of his skin and the sprinkling of fine dark hairs that curled above the V of his robe. 'I'm surprised she thought it was safe to leave you unchaperoned in the house with me,' she added sarcastically—and immediately wished she hadn't.

'And is it?' he challenged.

She glared at him. 'Absolutely, Mr Hartt.'

'How very disappointing,' he smiled. Then he leaned back slightly in his seat and regarded her tight-lipped face. 'How's business these days, now that the competition's closed down?'

She threw him a suspicious look. 'You mean to tell me Spinning Wheel Antiques is closed for good?'

He shrugged. 'I have no further use for it.'

'How come? I thought it was part of your plan?'

'I've changed my plan.' Slowly, he laid down his knife and fork. 'I decided that, after all, it wasn't really fair to make you suffer for Cole's sins. You're not and never have been involved. You finally convinced me of that.'

She held his eyes. 'What sins are you referring to? You're the one who's sinned, not Graham.'

'Your only crime,' he continued, totally ignoring her remark, 'has been to get involved with the wrong man. A regrettable folly, but hardly an indictable offence. I have no wish whatsoever for any damage to accrue to you.' And he paused to regard her with deeply mysterious, gold-flecked eyes. 'I sincerely hope that whatever damage was already done has now been satisfactorily accounted for.'

So she'd been right to recognise his hand in the mysterious purchase of the *secrétaire*. How easily he seemed to switch from the role of villain to that of benefactor—but he was in for a big disappointment if he expected gratitude. She stared across at him resentfully. 'So you could have saved yourself the trouble and expense of moving down here. I assume it was in order to oversee the destruction of Bridge Antiques from close at hand that you found yourself this little base.'

'Don't flatter yourself.' He dismissed the suggestion with a wave of his hand. 'I started negotiations for this house long before I knew that you and Cole were in the area. I bought it, quite simply, because I've always fancied a weekend retreat in Kent. The fact that the pair of you turned up just a matter of miles away was simply one of life's little coincidences—happy or otherwise, depending on one's point of view.' He threw her a stony look. 'I would guess that Cole thinks otherwise and that's why he's done a bunk.'

Jessica glared back at him. He was so damned arrogant, so utterly, infallibly sure of himself! He had an answer for everything. 'Spare me your theories,' she spat. 'Just tell me where he is.'

'Where I *think* he may be,' he corrected her.

She clenched her fists. 'And where is that?'

He very deliberately poured more coffee before answering. 'I believe he's hiding out somewhere in the West Midlands. A place called Warley, according to my sources.'

'According to your spies, you mean!'

He lifted the fine porcelain coffee-cup to his lips. 'Nothing so melodramatic as espionage as involved, dear Jessica. I simply refer to information received from a company of private investigators whose services I hire from time to time.'

'No doubt.' He most likely had dealings with all sorts of undesirables. 'So where exactly in Warley is Graham? What I need is an address.'

'And I'm sure I can lay hands on one easily enough.' He threw her a mocking smile, indicating with a gesture the current insubstantial manner of his dress. 'As you can see, I don't happen to have it on me right now—so I'm afraid you'll have to wait.' Then, anticipating the protest that was already springing to her lips, he raised one hand to silence her. 'All in good time, Jessica. You shall have what you want all in good time.' He paused. 'First, I shall endeavour once more to wipe the scales from your eyes and explain to you at the same time my special interest in Cole.'

'That should be interesting!' There was an undisguised sneer in Jessica's voice as she sat back expectantly in her seat. 'Go on, tell me the whole lurid story, the entire pack of filthy lies!' Though, in spite of her contempt, she did feel a spark of genuine curiosity—and an odd, uncomfortable foreboding that she fought to hide. Alas, perhaps not with complete success.

'I'm afraid you're not going to like it,' he said. 'You're not going to like it one little bit.' He folded his arms across his chest, so that the sleeves of the navy silk robe were pulled back, exposing strongly muscles forearms and powerfully sinewed wrists. 'But, I promise you, every word of it is true.' He sat back, the grey eyes boring into hers. 'First, a little background, just to illustrate what manner of individual we're dealing with. Some of this, of course, you had the opportunity to verify for yourself.' He paused. 'I refer to that list I supplied you with a few months ago.'

Jessica gave a derisive sniff. The list of people whom Graham had purportedly cheated in some way. 'I tore it up.' Precisely the fate the foul document deserved.

'You would have done better to avail yourself of the information it contained. If you had, you probably could have avoided the situation you're in now.' He went on without explaining the meaning of that remark. 'That list named only a few of his victims. There are many more. And they all fall within that category of people least able to defend themselves against a con-man like Cole. The old, the lonely and the vulnerable. That's who he preys upon. And that's why I despise him so much.'

He paused to ensure he had Jessica's full attention before going on. 'He presents himself to them in the guise of a good Samaritan, and then he proceeds to rob them blind.' The wide mouth curled in distaste. 'Let me give you an example of what I mean. One of his favourite methods of tracking down potential victims is through the obituary columns in local newspapers. An appropriate source for the vulture he is, and far less time-consuming than simply knocking at random on front doors. He waits till a decent interval has elapsed and then he turns up on the doorstep of the bereaved one day, and asks them if they have any antiques to sell.'

Jessica was staring at him, rigid with disbelief, but she made no effort to interrupt him as he carried on, 'A man or woman who has recently lost a spouse tends to be more suggestible, more lacking in judgement than they might be normally. And such a person may also suddenly find themselves in somewhat straitened circumstances. The idea of a quick sale of some old painting or piece of furniture may actually quite appeal to them. They find themselves listening—and, before they realise what they're doing, they've agreed to sell various bits and pieces to this stranger at a fraction of what the stuff is really worth.'

'That's despicable! Graham would never do such a thing!'

'Oh, he would, Jessica, I assure you. That was how he made his living before he met you. As I said—cheating the old, the lonely and the recently bereaved. He had a stall in an antiques emporium in South London where he used to sell the spoils. He's turned respectable over the past year or so. His old mates would scarcely recognise him. Mind you, they'd have a hard job tracking him down. He's changed his name more than a couple of times.'

It was a complete fairy story from start to finish. Surely Hartt didn't seriously expect her to believe a word of it? 'Graham had a share in an antiques shop in Truro before I met him,' she protested indignantly. 'The business went bust through absolutely no fault of his. His partners misappropriated some funds and Graham was left to foot the bill.'

'So that's the story he told you, is it? Did you ever bother to check it out?'

'Of course not!'

Hartt shook his head. 'Very unwise. You must learn not to be so trusting, Jessica.' Then with a knowledgeable glint in his granite-grey eyes, 'No doubt he borrowed money from you in the early days of your relationship—before his ambitions grew to include a partnership?' He paused significantly. 'I would also suspect that he has yet to pay for his share of the business.'

'But he did repay the money he borrowed!' Jessica defended at once, carelessly revealing that the allegations were true. She shifted uncomfortably in her chair. 'What have my private dealings with Graham to do with your ridiculous story, anyway?'

'I merely wish to illuminate what should already be obvious. That it's your money, your business, he's been after all along—not you.' He spoke the words cruelly, knowing how much they hurt, and paused to study her ashen face before adding on a malicious note, 'A quick profit's all he's ever been interested in.' The muscles around his jaw hardened vindictively. 'But he made a big mistake the day he knocked on a certain door in Rickmansworth.'

He paused and, just for a moment, a look of genuine sorrow flitted across his face. 'For the door he knocked on that unhappy day was the home of my parents' former housekeeper, old Mrs Penn. The very last person in the world who deserved to come a cropper at the hands of Cole.' He ran long fingers pensively around his clean-shaven jaw. 'She'd worked for my parents for more than twenty-five years, ever since her husband died. I grew up with her. She was part of the family. A lovely woman.

Kind-hearted, loyal, generous. Always eager to believe the best of her fellow men.' He swore softly. 'The perfect victim, in fact.'

Then he took a deep breath and continued, his eyes fixed on the tablecloth in front of him. 'When my parents retired to the South of France four years ago, Mrs Penn decided to retire to Rickmansworth. It was the part of the world where she was born, and she wanted to live out her last years there. My parents helped her to buy a house and set her up with a nice little investment that would pay enough interest for her to live on comfortably and provide a small inheritance for her nephew whom she doted on. In addition—and this, it turned out, was the fatal mistake they made—they made her a present of a number of paintings and antiques from their old London home, pieces that Mrs Penn had always particularly admired.'

His eyes flicked up suddenly to mesh with Jessica's. 'I don't know if he knew about the stuff or if it was just a coincidence, but one day Cole turned up on her doorstep, touting for business. Unfortunately, it happened to be right at a time when Mrs Penn was looking for extra cash. Just a few days earlier, she'd received a begging letter from that no-good nephew of hers. He'd got himself into some heavy debt—and, as usual, he expected her to get him out of it. She, of course, was prepared to go to any lengths to help him out. Cole, I imagine, had no great difficulty in persuading her to part with one of the paintings my parents had given her. A piece which could have settled her nephew's debts twice over, but for which Cole paid her only a miserable fraction of its worth.

'The saga continues.' Hartt straightened abruptly in his seat. The memories were clearly very painful for him. 'He talked her into selling him another couple of ornaments and things to make up the balance, then a little bureau, and when she refused to part with any more he persuaded her to lend him some of the more valuable pieces of furniture so that he could have them restored for her. Then, after doing absolutely nothing to them of course, because they were in perfect condition to start with, he landed her with a mountain of horrendous bills. I won't bore you with any more of the details, but by the time Cole had finished with that poor woman she'd been forced to eat into her capital to such an extent that the interest it rendered was barely enough to pay her rates.' He snatched the napkin from his lap and flung it across the table angrily. 'She was forced to sell her house in the end—the only home of her own she'd ever had in her entire life—and ended her days in virtual penury and failing health in some third-rate old people's home.'

He stood up abruptly and walked to the tall, bright window at the end of the room and stood staring out into the garden, his back to Jessica. 'She was too proud to turn to my parents for help. We only found out what had happened shortly before she died. And it was too late, then, to do anything.' A short, somehow ominous, pause, then he added in a low and deeply menacing voice, 'But it wasn't too late to make the bastard who was responsible pay for what he'd done to her. And that, dear Jessica, is the reason I'm after Cole.'

Jessica stared numbly at his broad back. It couldn't be! Surely that litany of greed and shameful inhumanity could have nothing to do with Graham. 'Mr Hartt, I just know you've made a terrible mistake,' she managed to tell him in a feeble voice. 'It's someone else you're after. Graham couldn't do what you've described.'

He swung round on her. 'Don't you believe it! He did it all right, and he's going to pay for it! If it's the very last thing I do, I'll see that blood-sucking bastard in hell. A hell that I intend to create personally for him. I may have backed off temporarily because of you, but, believe me, I'm far from finished with Cole. Before I'm through with him, he'll know what it feels like to have all of his possessions, even his dignity, stripped away. To see his dreams and all that he's worked for collapse in stinking ruins at his feet. He'll know what it feels like to be alone in the world, without hope, afraid, longing in the end for death. All that he inflicted on Mrs Penn I intend to make him suffer, too!'

He was standing in the middle of the room, fists clenched, his face a dark mask of rage. Like some avenging Fury from hell. And the unleashed anger in him sent a cold shiver down Jessica's spine. He looked almost capable of tearing the world apart with his bare hands right there and then. Yet, though she knew he was wrong about Graham, for the first time, she felt a glimmer of understanding for the man. Through the violent desire for revenge in him, there was something deeply moving about the strength of emotion that lay behind it all. He was suddenly less of a stranger somehow.

Shakily, Jessica rose to her feet. 'I understand how you must feel,' she said. 'It was a terrible thing to happen to someone you care about. But you're after the wrong man, I promise you. It can't have been Graham. It can't have been.'

Suddenly, all the anger seemed to drain out of him. He sighed and let his arms fall loosely to his sides. 'You're so damned loyal,' he said. 'I can't help admiring you for it, but it's such a waste.' Then, when she didn't answer him but just stood there watching him with a look of bewilderment and pain etched on her face, he shook his head. 'You know, the one thing that's surprised me in all this is that Cole didn't persuade you to accept my terms right at the start. I was absolutely sure he'd jump at that chance—solely in order to get his hands on as much of the settlement as possible, of course.' He smiled a wry smile. 'Then, when I had him right there in my clutches in the guise of his legitimate business partner, I could really have put the screws on him.' He thrust his hands into the pockets of his robe. 'But that didn't happen. How did you manage to resist the pressure he must have put on you?'

Jessica felt suddenly terribly exposed. Without even shifting from the spot, he seemed to be moving in on her. 'I didn't tell him,' she said.

He looked surprised. 'You didn't tell him about the offer I made?'

'I didn't tell him about any of it.' She wanted to take a step back, away from him, but she couldn't.

'Why ever not?'

'There wouldn't have been any point. It would only have upset him. And I knew all along that you were wrong.' She felt glued to the spot and her heart was fluttering nervously. 'Besides, I felt perfectly capable of handling the situation by myself.'

Hartt laughed. 'Good God, Jessica, you're so protective of the man!' He took a step forward, the dark eyes boring relentlessly into hers. 'Don't you know it's the male of the species who's supposed to protect the female, and not the other way around?'

All at once, she felt as though she could not breathe, her muscles turned to jelly, her pulses suddenly racing at twice their normal speed. With a great effort, she told him, 'I don't subscribe to that male-chauvinist theory. I'm perfectly able to look after myself.'

'I know. You've already told me so.' His hands slipped from his pockets and he reached out to grasp her lightly by the arms. 'Though you've yet to convince me of the truth of it.'

She wanted to break away from him—and it would have been so easy if she could only have found the willpower, the strength. He was barely holding on to her. But she just stood there, gazing helplessly back at him, feeling as though she were somehow being drawn into the fathomless dark pools of his eyes. Then it was too late to resist. She closed her eyes and shuddered as he bent to kiss her on the lips.

'Jessica, Jessica.' Ever so gently, he was pulling her close, and she could feel the warm male hardness of him through the thin silk of his robe, the firm pressure of his arms around her, enfolding her. She longed to sink against his chest, cling to him and yield to the clamour of sensations that his nearness aroused. To taste, without any holding back, the sweet excitement of his lips.

But she could not. Even as her arms ached to embrace the strong, hard shoulders and draw him even closer to her, and her fingers burned to reach up and gently caress the smooth, dark hair at the nape of his neck, her mind was willing her body to stiffen and draw away from him. This craving in her was madness! A betrayal of Graham. An even more unforgivable betrayal of herself.

Sensing the ambivalence in her, he released her with a sigh and softly smoothed the hair back from her face. 'What in God's name is a girl like you doing with a creep like Cole?'

It was precisely the provocation that she needed to respond. With sudden resolution, she pushed away from him. 'My relationship with Graham is really no concern of yours!' And on legs of cotton wool she walked back to the breakfast table and leaned against it gratefully. She took a deep breath. 'The only thing I want from you is his address.'

He cast a scathing eye over her flushed, excited face. 'You could have fooled me.' And he thrust his hands into the pockets of his robe again. 'I'll tell you one thing, Jessica. Whatever your relationship with Cole may be, it's not love, in spite of everything you say. No woman responds to a man the way that you just did when she's in love with someone else. You tried to fight it—and you won this time—but I could feel it all the same.'

'You bastard!' Her fingers clutched at the edge of the breakfast table that was supporting her. 'What are you talking about? You forced yourself on me!'

He shook his head at her and smiled a faintly condescending smile. 'You really are the master of self-deception, aren't you? But even you will come to your senses eventually.' He took a step forward, making her heart leap anxiously into her throat. 'I just hope you don't take too long. I'm already running out of self-restraint.'

'And what is that supposed to mean?' She pressed back against the table, vowing that if he took another step towards her she would scream.

But, instead, he paused and looked down on her with a scornful eye. 'It means that, just as soon as you're finished with Cole, I intend going after him again.'

She glared at him, resenting the way he had deliberately wrong-footed her. 'Is revenge really all you ever think about?' she demanded angrily.

'No, but it's enough to be going on with for now.' He turned abruptly away. 'You may find yourself in a similar frame of mind when you're finished checking your bank account.' Then he swung off angrily towards the door, informing her over his shoulder, 'I'm going upstairs to get dressed!' and very nearly walked straight into the grey-haired woman whom Jessica herself had almost collided with earlier on the stairs.

'Mr Hartt, there's an urgent call for you from London,' the woman said.

He managed to pull himself up in time. 'I'll take it my study,' he barked. 'Thank you.' Then he abruptly commanded Jessica, 'You wait here!' And stormed out of the room.

She had no intention of leaving, anyway. At least, not until she'd got what she'd come for. She sat down weakly and poured herself a cup of lukewarm coffee as, quickly and efficiently, the woman began to clear away the breakfast things.

'Shall I bring you fresh coffee?' the woman asked.

'No, thanks.' She shook her head. 'This will do fine.' Though she was beginning to wish she'd eaten a proper breakfast now. She felt suddenly quite shaky and faint, as the staggering awfulness of what Hartt had told her gradually began to sink in. Even that Graham could be associated by suspicion with such a thing was quite shocking enough. She could not bear to contemplate how she would feel if it were true.

Restlessly, she got to her feet as the grey-haired woman wheeled her laden trolley out the door, crossing over to the window and breathing in deeply, struggling to ease the sudden tension in her breast. Hartt's accusations were nothing but malicious lies. He was simply, as ever, seeking to poison her mind against Graham, endeavouring to justify his campaign of spite.

She gazed, frowning, at the blaze of flowerbeds that stretched down to a tall beech hedge, with the glimpse of tennis courts and smooth green lawns beyond. And fought to smother the ever more powerful anxiety that was growing inside her now. For somehow it was Hartt's crude accusation regarding her own feelings for Graham that she found most threatening of all. And she felt her cheeks burn and her lips go pale as his foul taunt echoed in her brain. 'No woman responds to a man the way that you just did when she's in love with someone else!' It was untrue! She *did* love Graham! Though a shiver ran through her, as she forced herself to recognise one truth that she could not deny. Neither Graham nor any other man had ever aroused in her the powerful emotions that she felt for Hartt.

In sudden confusion and alarm, she turned away from the window and stared into the empty room. It was total lunacy to feel the way she did for Hartt. The overwhelming intensity of emotion he awakened in her, the excitement, the longing, the warm, sharp keening of desire, were simply something she would have to overcome. They had no place in her life, no place at all. The very fact that the touch of his lips and the thrill of his arms about her felt so utterly natural, so totally right, was precisely why it was so wrong. He was her enemy— because he was Graham's. How could she have forgotten that?

He walked into the room, dressed now in a light grey suit, white shirt and blue silk tie, and she felt her treacherous heart skip a beat.

'I'll take you up to Bridge Antiques,' he said. 'Let's go.'

It seemed that his earlier ill humour had dissolved away. He appeared relaxed and totally in control once more. 'That won't be necessary,' she told him, hanging back. 'The van's outside.'

'Not any more.' He smiled that irritating smile. 'I've already arranged for one of my staff to drive it to the shop for you. You'll come with me.'

She glared at him. So he was issuing orders again! But, deliberately, she kept her cool. There was only one thing that really mattered, after all. 'Did you get Graham's address for me?'

He slipped a folded paper from his pocket and waved it tantalisingly at her. 'Yes, Jessica. It's right here.'

She stepped forward and tried to snatch it from his hand, but he was too quick for her. In a flash, he had caught her by the wrist with his free hand, and the unexpected touch of him was like fire burning into her flesh.

The dark eyes smouldered down at her, teasing, amused. 'Patience, Jessica, patience! Don't be in such a hurry all the time.'

Face flaming, she pulled her hand away and followed him in silence to the door, consciously keeping her distance from him as he led her swiftly down the hall. How had he managed to win every single confrontation with her, hands down? What was this uncanny knack he had of always outsmarting her?

A dark blue Rolls Royce Silver Spirit was waiting outside for them. As he pulled open the passenger door for her, he smiled enigmatically. 'Much more comfortable for long journeys than the Porsche.'

She climbed inside the vast, leather-scented interior. 'I take it you're going up to London?' she asked.

'My presence is required there briefly to sort out a small problem that's cropped up.' He slammed the door shut and came round to the driver's side, slid in beside her and started the engine up. 'First, however,' he told her, shifting quickly into gear, 'we'll stop off at your shop.'

She threw him a suspicious sideways glance. 'What do you mean, "we"?'

The car moved forward soundlessly. 'I mean that I'll wait for you while you pick up a couple of things for the journey north.'

Jessica felt her spine stiffen with alarm. 'There's no need for you to wait. Just give me Graham's address and be on your way.'

'Oh, no.' He shook his head slowly, as the Rolls nosed out of the driveway and into the traffic of the main road. 'That would never do.' And he turned his penetrating gold-flecked eyes on her as the big car started to accelerate along the road. 'You're not going after Cole alone. I'm coming with you—whether you want me to or not!'

CHAPTER SIX

THE look on Deirdre's face when Jessica walked into Bridge Antiques with Luke Hartt at her heels was almost enough to make Jessica smile. From the gasp of admiration and the way her mouth dropped open in sheer surprise, you'd have thought her boss had no less a prize than the Prince of Wales himself in tow! But Jessica was feeling far from amused as she briefly introduced the two of them, then hurried upstairs to her little flat above the shop to change. Luke Hartt had manipulated her into yet another corner, it seemed.

She had offered her friend only the scantiest of explanations as to what was going on—there would be plenty of time to go into details when she got back—though she could tell that Deirdre was dying of curiosity. And no wonder. Hadn't Jessica just admitted to spending the night at Hartt's place? And wasn't she this very minute packing an overnight bag and preparing to go off to the Midlands with him? But if Deirdre was thinking what the gleam in her eye had seemed to suggest, she couldn't have been further from the truth. This was destined to be no pleasure trip, and Hartt's insistence on accompanying her would only make the ordeal worse.

The trouble was, she had no choice. 'Either you go with me or you don't go at all,' he told her when she'd tried to protest. '*I* have Cole's address. *You* don't. It's as simple as that.'

She'd glared at him. 'What do you want to go for, anyway? Are you out to make more trouble for Graham? Haven't you already done enough?'

'No, as a matter of fact, I haven't,' he'd answered predictably. 'But to make trouble, as you put it, isn't why I plan to come. Let's just say, I have my reasons and leave it at that.'

She didn't bother to press him as to what those reasons might be. He wouldn't have told her, and maybe it was better that way. He did seem to have rather an unhappy knack of telling her things she didn't really want to hear.

Angrily now, she stuffed a nightdress and sponge-bag into her travel bag and yanked the zipper shut. As much as she would have preferred to travel up to Warley and back to Kent all in the same day, she doubted very much that that would be possible. Though, in any event, she intended to lose Hartt just as soon as she'd located Graham. For one thing, she was anxious to speak in private to her fiancé. For another, the less time she spent in Luke Hartt's company, the happier she would feel.

She glanced quickly round the room, checking that she'd packed all she would need, then froze in sudden indecision as her eyes fell on the telephone. She could hear Hartt's warning ringing uncomfortably in her ears: 'I suggest you check your business account. I think you'll find that whatever funds you had in it have unaccountably disappeared.' She hated herself for even considering the base remark, yet she longed for reassurance that he was wrong. She steeled herself. It wouldn't do any harm to check.

Suddenly nervous, she picked up the receiver and dialled. 'Put me through to the business accounts manager,' she said. 'I want to check the current state of my account.' Then she held her breath and waited, praying that her mind would be set at rest on this, at least.

A few minutes later, as she laid down the phone with a trembling hand, she knew it was even more urgent than ever that she speak to Graham without delay.

They were on the highway, heading for London in no time at all. Jessica sat back in the leather-upholstered passenger seat of the Rolls—as deep and luxurious as an armchair—and tried to pull herself together. She felt shaken and bewildered by what she'd just learnt. It was monstrous! According to her bank manager, early on Friday morning Graham had completely cleaned out the firm's bank account. The weekend's takings, a few hundred pounds, were all the money she had left in the world.

Hartt seemed quite oblivious of his passenger's devastated state of mind. He had shed his jacket before they set out, tossed it casually in the back seat and pushed back the sleeves of his crisp white shirt. 'Do you mind if we listen to some music?' he'd asked, switching on a Beethoven sonata before she even had time to reply.

Not that she minded in the least. The music was soothing, and it provided her with the perfect excuse for keeping quiet. Right now, conversation was the last thing she felt capable of. But, as he reached out suddenly to turn the volume down, it occurred to her that she should have guessed he wouldn't leave her in peace for long.

'Everything OK, Jessica?'

'Fine. Fine.' She straightened abruptly and forced what she hoped was a convincing smile. She had no intention of discussing this latest treacherous blow with him. Wouldn't he just love to discover he'd been absolutely right again!

'Good. I thought you seemed a little quiet.'

'Just listening to the music,' she lied, glancing round at the mysterious dark profile at her side. For the next twenty-four hours or so, she'd have to stay on her toes.

But his next remark made her relax a bit. 'Seems like a nice girl, that assistant of yours. Has she been with you long?'

'Since the beginning,' she replied, wondering if he realised that the admiration had been mutual. There had been no mistaking the look of unqualified approval in Deirdre's normally clear-sighted eyes. 'I more or less inherited her with the business.' Then she added hastily, lest her answer sound ungracious towards her friend, 'Over the years, she's been worth her weight in gold. I could never have managed without her, quite honestly.'

'So she worked for your aunt, did she?' He turned to her briefly, the bronzed hands resting lightly on the steering wheel. 'Is she a local girl?'

'Yes, she's from Harbingdon. She was with my aunt for seven years. There isn't very much that Deirdre doesn't know about the antiques trade.'

A smile that was plainly provocative flickered across the handsome lips. 'You should have made her your partner, not Cole.'

Jessica's eyes narrowed with hostility. Trust him to get in the perpetual dig! Besides, he was getting far too close for comfort now. For the moment, Graham was a subject she'd prefer to avoid. 'I can't see what business it is of yours whom I choose to make my partner!' she retorted, and turned away, hoping he'd be prepared to let the matter rest.

But he hadn't quite finished yet. 'I couldn't agree more,' he told her, turning his eyes back to the road. 'But it does seem a pity you couldn't have chosen someone a little more dependable. And Deirdre most definitely struck me as being that.' He flicked a look across at her. 'She also struck me as having a great deal of common sense and a fine sense of judgement. Throughout the fifteen or so minutes I spent with her, she never stopped singing your praises.' Then he killed the unexpected compliment by adding, to annoy her, 'However, she doesn't think so highly of Cole, does she?'

Jessica spun round indignantly in her seat. 'Were you discussing Graham with Deirdre while I was upstairs? You have no right! You have no right at all to discuss my private affairs with anyone!'

He shook his head at her and smiled. 'Calm down, Jessica. Calm down. Even if I'd wanted to, I'm sure that Deirdre is much too loyal to oblige. But the subject of Cole did, quite naturally, arise. I gathered, more from what she didn't rather than did say, that she had no great admiration for the man.'

'So what? It happens. Sometimes, people just don't get along. It's nobody's fault.' Though it had always slightly upset Jessica the way Deirdre could be so impatient, so scathing of Graham.

She turned her eyes irritably back to the road. 'Anyway, I don't wish to discuss it. In fact, I'd really rather not discuss anything with you.'

'Suit yourself.'

As he leaned forward unconcernedly and turned up the volume of the cassette, Jessica hunched her shoulders and stared out moodily at the road. He was wrong about Graham. And Deirdre was, too. And in spite of the way things looked right now, Graham would prove it, she told herself. Just as soon as he had an opportunity to defend himself.

It was just gone twelve when they drove into the underground car park of the Minerva building overlooking the Thames. A man with a gold stripe down the side of his uniform trousers, and a matching stripe above the brim of his smart peaked cap, greeted Hartt with a cheerful salute. 'Good morning, Mr Hartt, sir!'

'Good morning, Reeves.' He pulled on his jacket and tossed the car keys to the man. 'Have her tanked up and ready for a long journey in a couple of hours,' he told him, and strode off, with Jessica behind him, towards the lift.

The man beamed and saluted again. 'Right you are, sir, Mr Hartt. I'll have her ready for you, have no fear.' He was apparently delighted to be of service to his boss.

And this willing, enthusiastic response was what Jessica observed repeatedly in the course of their journey up to the executive offices on the fifteenth floor, from messenger boys and junior managers and senior secretaries alike. She gazed, askance, at Hartt as he strode ahead of her through the palatial

outer office of his own private suite. Either his
entire staff were uncannily well drilled—or Hartt
really was a singularly well liked and respected boss.

He turned to address her. 'I'm going to be busy
for the next couple of hours, so you have a choice.
Either you can sit here in my office and get
thoroughly bored, or you can join one of the secretaries for lunch in the canteen. My own secretary,
alas,' he added with a wicked smile, 'will be unable
to look after you. She's out on an errand, I
understand.'

Well, that was something to be grateful for! Two
hours in the hatchet-faced company of Miss Clutton
was not something Jessica would have relished
much. 'I'll opt for the lunch.' After the self-imposed
frugality of breakfast, she was feeling decidedly in
need of sustenance.

And lunch was delicious. This was no ordinary
canteen, Jessica observed, eyeing the mouth-
watering variety of dishes on display. It wasn't too
difficult to believe what her companion, Laura, was
at great pains to point out—that Hartt himself
lunched here, not infrequently.

Of course, Laura, as Jessica quickly realised, had
nothing but good to say for the man. So Jessica
listened politely and kept her own, rather different,
feelings to herself. These, she felt intuitively, would
be totally out of context here. To the devoted young
secretary whom Hartt had detailed to accompany
her, it would probably have sounded as though she
were talking about a different man.

'He demands a great deal of his staff,' the girl
told her over mushroom quiche and *salade Niçoise*.
'But in return he treats us generously—and he's fair.

Once they've landed a job with Minerva, people tend to want to stay. There are some who've been with the company virtually from the start.'

'Like Miss Clutton, no doubt?'

Laura smiled an indulgent smile. 'You know Miss Clutton, do you?'

'We've met.'

'She's Mr Hartt's right hand, you know.' The girl leaned forward confidentially. 'He always says he'd be totally lost if Miss Clutton ever left.'

Jessica sniffed. Hartt, lost? A highly unlikely notion, indeed.

The indispensable Miss Clutton was back behind her desk by the time Jessica returned to the fifteenth floor. 'Mr Hartt is still occupied,' she informed the intruder with a glassy stare. 'I'm afraid you'll just have to wait. He'll be another hour at least.'

'Do you think he'd mind if I had a look round the building while I'm waiting?' Jessica asked, partly because she was genuinely curious, but primarily because she was anxious to escape from the woman's relentlessly disapproving stare. Did she still believe that Jessica was making a play for Hartt?

Judging by her answer, it seemed she did. 'I can't see any objection—just so long as you're not planning to pay a visit to the penthouse, of course.'

'The penthouse?' Jessica met her eyes with an uncomprehending stare.

'Mr Hartt's private apartment. I think it would be preferable if you didn't stray as far as there.'

She glared at the woman. 'I don't think that particular part of the building would be of any interest to me,' she retorted stiffly, though she smiled to herself as she set off on her tour. So, just like herself, Luke Hartt lived over the shop!

Though it was some shop. An impressive, multi-million dollar, eighteen-storey block. For Minerva was much more than just a property company, as Jessica already knew. Housed within the ultra-modern tower block were the headquarters of many of its dozens of subsidiaries—in fields as diverse as insurance, fashion, industrial chemicals and advertising. And there was something severely daunting as well as hugely impressive about it all. A man who was capable of building for himself an empire such as this from the modest beginnings of a run-down property in Lewisham must surely be capable of almost anything. Perhaps, after all, that was why Graham had disappeared, she found herself surmising bitterly. He'd recognised all too plainly the devil he was up against.

In the end, she did spend an uncomfortable couple of hours in Miss Clutton's company, flicking disinterestedly through a pile of commercial magazines while the thin-faced woman clicked away like an automaton at the keys of her word processor. It was after five by the time Hartt finally appeared, with only the most perfunctory of apologies, and informed her, 'OK, let's go. I want to get there before dark.'

Jessica followed him mutely along the corridor to the lift, deliberately biting back the complaints she'd intended making about having been left to wait so long. Whatever problems he'd been required to deal with over the past few hours had cast a shadow of strained fatigue over his face. As the lift doors closed, she glanced up at the distinctly weary-looking figure in the charcoal suit and reflected with vindictive pleasure how hard it must sometimes be at the top.

Down in the car park, Reeves was waiting by the Rolls. He tipped his cap and handed the keys to Hartt. 'Safe journey, sir.'

'Thank you.' Hartt strode round to the driver's door as Reeves helped Jessica into the passenger seat. And he glanced at his watch as he snapped his seat-belt into place. 'If the traffic's not too bad, we should be in Birmingham in time for dinner.'

Jessica eyed him. 'If you don't mind, I'd rather just skip dinner and go straight on to Warley to find Graham.'

'Well, I'm afraid *I* wouldn't.' His tone was sharp, discouraging further argument. 'Unlike you, I've had nothing but a sandwich since breakfast,' he said.

A sharp stab of frustration made her react. They'd already wasted so much time. 'You promised to take me straight to Graham.'

The pinch of fatigue around his jaw sharpened to irritation now. 'I promised no such thing.' He turned away from her dismissively and started the engine up. 'We'll spend the night in Birmingham and go after Cole first thing tomorrow morning. Don't worry, he'll still be there.'

'I don't care. I want to go and find him tonight.'

'Well, that's too bad.' The grey eyes snapped round impatiently. 'Now, kindly just buckle up and spare me the arguments. Otherwise——' as she opened her mouth to make one final protest '—I'll drive you straight back to Harbingdon and let you find Cole for yourself, if you can.'

Seething, and knowing that he meant every word of his threat, Jessica snapped the seat-belt into place and glowered at him.

'Good girl.' He smiled sarcastically as they headed out into the street. 'I've booked us into a hotel. I think you should find it to your taste.'

The exclusive five-star hotel, a few miles outside Birmingham itself, in the city's new conference complex, was a great deal flashier than anything Jessica was accustomed to. Its unashamed opulence was something that, in other circumstances, she knew she could quite easily learn to enjoy, but not tonight. And not with Hartt. There were too many worries cluttering her mind to allow any real enjoyment of anything.

Rooms had been reserved for them—on the same floor, but at opposite ends of a long corridor. Good, thought Jessica as she unpacked her few things and ran a relaxing bubble bath. At least she wouldn't have Hartt breathing down her neck throughout the duration of their stay. Though there was no way she could get out of dinner with him. He had insisted on that.

She had brought only a couple of dresses with her—one a slim blue cotton-jersey sheath. With a wide black belt at her waist, matching shoes and her shoulder-length chestnut hair piled on her head, she felt she wouldn't look too informal amid the other diners in the big, elegantly decorated dining-room. In fact, as she and Luke made their way together between the crowded tables to a well placed corner table at the back, virtually every pair of eyes in the room turned to follow them admiringly. Separately, the tall, dark-haired man with his powerful, impressive bearing and expensively tailored charcoal suit, and the slender, sensuously striking girl in blue would have turned heads, anyway. Together, they sent a stir of whispered approval buzzing round the room.

A waiter took their orders and aperitifs were brought. And it was evident, from the nods and smiles of greeting and the speedy, immaculate service, that Hartt was known to the hotel staff.

'Don't tell me you own the hotel as well,' Jessica remarked caustically, raising the perfectly mixed Martini to her lips. 'These people bow and scrape to you almost as much as they do at Minerva.' It was an unfair gibe, but the way that everything always seemed to fall into place for him was beginning to grate a little on her nerves.

He was totally unruffled by the barb, of course. 'I suppose my face is known in quite a few hotels around the world,' he answered. 'I tend to travel quite a lot.'

'And no doubt pay for your popularity everywhere by handing out enormous tips. Buying people is your stock in trade.'

He merely smiled a superior smile. 'I've yet to have any complaints,' he said. 'In my experience, people are more highly motivated by the promise of financial reward than by other, perhaps more noble, forms of recompense.' He shrugged. 'Can I help it if human nature is what it is?'

Jessica fingered her glass. Her taunts merely amused him. The man had an answer for everything. She leaned back in her chair and crossed one long, slim leg over the other. 'Well, I would hate to live like you,' she told him cuttingly. 'Surrounded everywhere you go by sycophants and hangers-on.'

'Well, you should know.' He raised one dark eyebrow at her. 'About hangers-on, I mean. I think that is a not inaccurate way of describing Cole.'

Jessica glared across at him. He never lost an opportunity! 'Graham is my fiancé and my business partner. I don't think that description fits him at all.'

'In spite of the fact that he's just run off with all the loot?' The grey eyes narrowed. 'Don't try to deny it, Jessica. I saw your face when you came down those stairs from your flat to the shop. You'd just phoned your bank manager, hadn't you? You looked as though you'd seen a ghost.'

So his eyes were sharper than she gave him credit for. As a waiter appeared with perfect timing and laid duck pâté in front of her, she stared down at her plate, avoiding Hartt's eyes. She waited till the wine had been poured before answering, 'I'm sure there's a perfectly plausible reason for that. It will all become clear tomorrow when I have a chance to speak to Graham.' Hollow as it sounded, even to her own ears, to believe otherwise would be like sticking a knife right through her heart. It was totally inconceivable that Graham could steal from her. He was the man she had promised to marry. How could he be capable of anything so foul?

Hartt was looking across at her with total scepticism in his eyes. 'I hate to say this,' he said, 'but I fear you're in for a nasty shock tomorrow—in more ways than one.' He lifted his napkin from the table and shook it across his lap. 'But let's not ruin our appetites by discussing Cole. Let's just try to enjoy the meal and leave tomorrow to take care of itself.'

Jessica refrained from asking what he'd meant by "in more ways than one". It was typical of the man to pile on the agony, to try to make her even more afraid than she already was! With a resolute toss of her head, she reached for a slice of melba toast. At least his advice to try and enjoy the meal made sense. 'If you'll keep off the subject, so will I,' she promised with a wooden smile. Then her eyes flicked up aggressively to mesh with his. 'In fact, if you refer to the subject again, I'll get up and leave.' He wasn't the only one who could make threats!

A smile curled at the corners of his lips. 'We can't have that,' he offered condescendingly. And raised his wine glass to her in a mock-toast. 'Here's to a truce, then. *Bon appetit!*'

Half-way through the meal, a small band set up in a corner of the room and proceeded to play discreetly, lending an air of romance and informality to the atmosphere. One or two couples got up to dance, and as she watched them Jessica was struck by how far removed she had become lately from the normal social pleasures of life. She had never been a great club- or party-goer, but she had always enjoyed dressing up and going out in company. Even during the days when most of her energies had been devoted to building up the business, she had still managed to find time for the occasional date.

When Graham had come on the scene, of course, the pace of her social life had increased dramatically—though in the last six months it had diminished somewhat. Graham seemed to spend more and more weekends away from home on buying trips. And, latterly, things had come to a virtual dead halt. Neither she nor Graham seemed to be in the mood for enjoying themselves very much these days. She glanced resentfully across at Hartt. It was all his fault. He was the one who had turned her whole life on its head.

She had followed his advice on the entrée—exquisite steak *béarnaise*—and decided, again on his recommendation, on *crêpes Suzette* for dessert.

'There's only one person in the world who makes *crêpes Suzette* better than they do here,' he told her, 'and that's my mother.' In the flame of the burner, as the waiter worked his magic at their tableside, the lines of his face were softened, his fatigue now evidently gone, and the dark eyes looked out at her through lashes that seemed shamefully long.

Deliberately, Jessica looked away. 'She's French, isn't she?' she commented lightly as the waiter slid two thin pancakes on to a plate and laid it down in front of her. 'Annette told me last night.'

'She's from Paris. She met my father while she was working as a court reporter for *Le Monde*. He was defending some case at the Old Bailey, involving a couple of French nationals.'

She threw him a teasing smile. 'I hope he managed to get them off.'

'Of course.' He smiled back at her. 'He was most anxious to impress my mother, you see.'

Jessica waited until he'd been served, then took a spoonful of the *crêpe* with its sweet, brandied sauce. 'Well, if she can make better *crêpes* than these, I'd say that she was worth impressing.'

Luke was watching her with interest. He smiled. 'Besides, he really didn't have much choice. My mother refused to go out with him unless he won the case. And she's very good at getting her way.'

Like mother, like son. 'And did you inherit any of her talents, by any chance?'

'I'm a fair cook,' he answered, though she could tell from the glint of amusement in his eyes that he had understood perfectly what she'd been getting at. 'My *boeuf bourguignonne* has been very highly recommended in its time.'

Jessica laughed. Somehow the image of Luke Hartt in the kitchen, messing around with garlic and frying-pans, lacked serious credibility. 'I don't believe you for a minute. Your highly recommended *boeuf bourguignonne* undoubtedly came from the local high-class caterers.'

'Not a bit of it,' he protested, still watching her. 'I quite enjoy a bit of culinary exercise occasionally.'

'I'll bet!' she joked, meeting his eyes. '*Very* occasionally!'

He leaned back a little in his seat. 'Surely you're not one of those women who don't think a man should know how to cook? I had you figured for a little more liberated than that.'

He was pulling her leg, of course. 'Don't worry, I'm liberated enough,' she assured him with a good-humoured smile. 'It's just that I can't quite see a man with your male-chauvinist tendencies indulging in some domesticity.'

The dark eyes surveyed her thoughtfully. 'Well, as it happens Jessica, you're wrong. At heart, I'm a very domestic animal indeed.' Then he paused for a moment before adding, 'If you and I were on better terms, I'd invite you round for a home-cooked meal some time and let you judge for yourself. About a number of things.'

Illogically, Jessica felt her colour rise. She dropped her eyes to her plate and laid down her spoon. 'I'm sorry,' she protested. 'I don't think I could manage another bite.'

'Don't worry. We'll have coffee now.' And he smiled, lightening the suddenly loaded atmosphere, then summoned the waiter with a flick of his hand. 'Bring coffee and two brandies, please.'

Jessica glanced cautiously across at him. Perhaps she'd already had enough to drink. In the course of the meal, she'd consumed her share of a vintage bottle of Pommard, and there was no denying it had gone, ever so slightly, to her head. Why else would it be that she almost felt as though she were enjoying herself? 'Make mine a very small one,' she amended hurriedly.

The waiter moved off and, all at once, Luke was rising to his feet. He reached out a hand and stood for a moment, looking down at her. 'Come on, Jessica,' he said. 'Let's dance.'

She hesitated. Dance? She was on the point of refusing, of shaking her head, but his hand was suddenly on her arm, guiding her to her feet. And, as though she were in a trance, she found herself responding to his unspoken command. Then his arm was firmly around her waist, propelling her on to the dance-floor, and she felt as though she was floating on air.

The band was playing an up-tempo number, she registered dimly, unconsciously grateful for the fact. Just the touch of his hand against her waist was quite unsettling enough.

'You dance well,' she heard him say from what sounded like a long way off. 'We should have done this before.'

And she heard herself laugh in light-hearted response. 'I always dance better after a three-course meal!' She half wondered if she had suddenly taken leave of her senses. Surely she oughtn't to be dancing with Luke Hartt? She should be sitting dolefully upstairs in her room, alone. It was madness. But she didn't want to stop.

Abruptly, the tempo slowed, and before she could react and step away—though she knew in her heart she would probably not have done so, anyway—his arms had folded around her, drawing her close. And something quickened inside her as she felt the hard thighs brushing against hers, the warm, enveloping pressure of the strong, muscular chest, and she longed just to close her eyes and let her senses drift away with her.

It wasn't just the wine and the music and the night. It was this feeling of rightness when she was close to him. This almost irresistible compulsion to let herself become a part of him.

As his arms tightened against her back, she sighed. And her heart broke into a nervous gallop as his chin came down to rest against her cheek and she felt his warm breath ruffle her hair. Her hands were laid lightly on his shoulders, though they longed to encircle his neck, and the muscles in her legs seemed to dissolve as his head turned just a fraction and she felt his lips brush softly against her face.

'Jessica,' he whispered. Then his lips were moving towards hers, and she knew she had to break away. Her stomach was in turmoil. She could scarcely breathe. But, instead, she closed her eyes and tilted her face towards him helplessly, shuddering as she felt his mouth close over hers and his fingers slide against the silky tresses of her hair, urging her lips into firmer contact with his.

It was like a fire rushing through her. The warm, exciting pressure of his mouth on hers, the touch of his strong hand, firm against her back, the sharp, sweet thrill of intimacy as his tongue flicked lightly against her teeth. But she must not succumb! In sudden alarm, her fingers stiffened against his shoulders and she struggled to pull away from him. 'No, Luke!'

'But why? he frowned, as his fingers continued to caress her neck.

She would have melted back into his arms if she had not summoned all her strength. 'We'd better go back,' she insisted, suddenly guilty and confused and filled with an overpowering regret. It was cruel that this man should be the one to make her feel this way, when the man to whom she was promised had no such power. She forced herself to look at him. 'Our coffee will be getting cold.'

He smiled. 'Let it. We can order more.'

But she dared not run the risk of staying here so close to him. Her resolve was really not that strong. 'I think I'd rather sit down now.'

'As you wish.' Almost formally, he took her by the hand, his clasp cool as he led her back to their table and sat down after her. And, as he released her, the space between them felt oddly unnatural and chill. Like the unexpected blast of winter through an autumn door.

A glass of brandy and a cup of coffee had been set down at either place. Blindly, Jessica reached for her cup and drank. Perhaps the strong brew would restore her to her senses, sober her up and stop her behaving like a fool. For that was precisely what she had done just then, acted like some kind of lunatic. And it must never, never happen again.

'Jessica?'

She glanced up at him nervously, wondering what he was about to say.

'Don't go tomorrow, Jessica.' The expression in the dark grey eyes was earnest, almost pleading, as he went on, 'Forget about Cole. I promise you're only going to wind up regretting it if you go to him.'

What was that supposed to mean? She took a deep breath. 'I haven't come all this way just to go home again. Of course I'm going to see Graham— and don't try to stop me. I've got to speak to him.'

'What about, for heaven's sake?' Sudden impatience flared in his eyes. 'He's taken your money and gone off and left you without a word. What further proof do you need of the sort of bastard he is?' And his hands clenched into angry fists on the table-top. 'What can you possibly have to talk to him about?'

'Everything.' He was trying to push her into a corner again, and she would not let him do it. Her mind was absolutely determined on that. 'I want to hear from Graham's own lips why he took the money—and what he has to say in answer to all those awful things that you've accused him of. I think he has a right to defend himself.' And somehow convince her, she prayed, that he was not the man Hartt said he was.

'You're a fool, Jessica. Don't you already know in your heart that there's no defence for what he's done?' And when she dropped her eyes abruptly from his, he spread his long fingers out on the tablecloth and sighed, a gesture of compromise. 'Look, I'm prepared to make it easy for you. Tell me how much money Cole's stolen from you and I'll pay you back every last penny of it. That way, you can forget about him without taking a financial loss.' He reached into his inside breast pocket as he went on, 'I'll write you a cheque right now, if you like.' And slipped the cap from a slim gold pen. 'Do yourself a favour, Jessica. Take this opportunity to save yourself a lot of heartache and finally get shot of him. For God's sake, don't throw yourself away on that piece of scum.'

'Don't try to tell me what to do—and don't try to buy me, Hartt!' In one violent movement, she was on her feet, sending the contents of her brandy glass flying across the tablecloth and very nearly toppling her chair to the floor. 'I don't want your money and I don't want your advice!' she spat. 'So don't bother trying to interfere with my life any more! You've already done more than enough damage!'

Then, before he could stop her, she had swung indignantly away and was walking stiffly from the room. However, she felt far from triumphant, but rather as if she were stumbling from a high cliff edge into the jaws of some dark and terrifying void.

For, already, some sixth sense was warning her of the calamity that lay ahead, and of how she would live to bitterly regret the decision that she'd just made.

CHAPTER SEVEN

THEY set out for Warley next morning, barely on speaking terms. Jessica had taken breakfast early in her room, having scarcely slept a wink all night, and she was already packed and waiting when Luke called through to tell her, 'Meet me down in the lobby in half an hour.'

She spent the next twenty minutes nervously pacing her room, then hurried anxiously downstairs and sat fidgeting in the reception area, impatient for him to arrive so she could get on with the ordeal she was somehow certain lay ahead.

He appeared at her elbow, making her start. 'I hope I didn't keep you waiting long. I indulged in rather a large breakfast, I'm afraid.' He was dressed casually in sand-coloured trousers and a burgundy shirt, and his tone as he surveyed her with those cool grey eyes was oddly detached and indifferent.

Already, Jessica was on her feet. 'That's OK. I was early.' Though she knew there was no call to explain. He wasn't really interested.

He reached out and took the small overnight bag from her hand, his fingers brushing lightly against hers, so that she stiffened and snatched her hand away, a childish reaction which irritated her, but of which he seemed oblivious. He turned away. 'Let's get on the road,' he said.

She followed his tall figure to the door, incongruously aware of the strong, broad back, the suntanned forearms below the partially rolled-back sleeves of his burgundy shirt. As he stood aside to let her pass through the automatic doors ahead of him, it struck her that he was probably the most handsome man she'd ever seen. She mentally chastised herself for such a thought—almost indecently out of context in the circumstances. The only man who should be on her mind right now was Graham. For nothing was more important at this point than the explanation he would have for her when she finally confronted him in just over an hour.

Almost as though it were programmed, the Rolls drew up alongside them the instant Hartt stepped through the door. The uniformed bell-hop at the wheel climbed out and hurried round to open the passenger door for Jessica. Then he quickly stowed her bag in the cavernous boot, beside Hartt's, before pocketing the folded bill Luke almost absent-mindedly handed him. Jessica smoothed her slim white skirt over her knees and smiled a wry smile to herself. As usual, power and money were oiling the wheels and everything was going just like clockwork for him.

He turned to look at her as they moved away. 'You're sure you want to go ahead with this? There's still time to change your mind, you know.' But it was spoken in the manner of one who already knows what the answer will be—and who no longer greatly cares.

Jessica stared straight ahead. 'I've no intention of changing my mind,' she told him flatly.

'So be it.' He leaned forward and switched some music on. Mozart. And it struck Jessica as she sat there stiffly, avoiding his eyes, that something a little more sombre might have been more in keeping with her mood. For, try as she might, she could not dispel the leaden feeling of doom that had crept into the cold, dark recesses of her heart.

It was not very far to Warley. Hartt drove confidently through the busy traffic, consulting no more than a brief couple of times the directions that were printed on the slip of paper with Graham's address. It was just after ten when he turned into a narrow street, very deliberately turning to look at her as he switched the car engine off.

'I think it would probably be a good idea if we parked here.'

Jessica felt the knot of apprehension in the pit of her stomach pull tight. 'Is this the place?'

He handed her the slip of paper. 'It's just round the corner,' he told her, pointing. 'Number forty-three. But I'll wait for you here. I think this car might be a little bit conspicuous in the circumstances.'

They were parked in a typical grey suburban street, lined with nondescript semi-detached houses, each with a neat little garden in front. So this was it. She reached for the door-handle, forcibly reminding herself that this was the moment she'd been so impatient for. But that did nothing to calm the butterflies beating like bats' wings in her stomach now. 'You don't have to wait,' she told him, safe in the certainty that, however much he disapproved of what she was doing, he would.

But he didn't answer as she stepped out on to the pavement, suddenly very much aware that she was on her own. And her limbs seemed to be moving mechanically as she started to slam the car door shut. In just a matter of minutes, she would know the truth.

'Good luck.' He leaned forward unexpectedly and caught the door lightly with his hand. Jessica had to snatch her eyes abruptly from the dark gaze and turn away. He mustn't see the fear in her. The utter, almost overwhelming sense of dread. For she knew that, if what he had told her proved to be true, she would never be able to trust anyone again as long as she lived.

Number forty-three was about half-way down the street, a drab-looking edifice with net curtains at the windows and a lemon-yellow-painted front door. Squaring her shoulders determinedly, Jessica pushed open the iron gate and marched briskly up the path, laid her finger on the doorbell and delivered two sharp rings. Then held her breath and waited for Graham to appear.

'Yes?' It was a young woman, a year or two older than herself, with tightly permed hair, and a plastic apron at her waist.

She had the wrong house! Relief and elation swept through her as she realised that Hartt had got his facts wrong, after all. She stepped back and threw the woman an apologetic smile. 'Sorry to disturb you. I must have the wrong address. I was looking for a Mr Graham Cole.' And she was about to turn away with almost indecent haste as a smile of something akin to amusement flitted across the woman's face.

'Mr Graham Cole, you say?' The tone was mocking, the voice hard. 'You must be one of his friends from down south.' And she screwed up her face as realisation slowly dawned. 'Don't tell me you're the little fiancée—Jessica Langley from Kent?'

Jessica's mouth dropped open. 'Is Graham here?'

The woman took a step back into the narrow hall and ostentatiously waved her inside. 'You could say that. Come in. He'll be quite delighted to see you, I'm sure.' Then she turned and bellowed up the stairs. 'Brian! Come down! You've got a visitor!'

Jessica followed hesitantly as the woman led the way into a small sitting-room, modestly but pleasantly furnished, and accepted the invitation to seat herself on a hard green chair. Who was this woman? How did she know who Jessica was? And why had she just called Graham "Brian"?

The woman remained standing, leaning with her back against a sideboard, looking down at her guest. 'Well, I must say,' she offered with an insolent smile, 'he was certainly telling the truth about one thing, for a change. You are a classy little piece.'

Jessica shifted uncomfortably in her chair. The situation was becoming more bizarre. She glanced up at the woman with a withering look. 'Who are you, anyway?' she asked.

Again, the oddly insolent smile as the woman laid her hands on her ample hips. 'Me? Oh, I'm no one special.' And her eyes fixed Jessica's with a look of triumph, as she added with a flippant smile, 'I'm just his wife, that's all.'

It was precisely at that moment that Graham walked through the door. He was unshaven and looked as though he'd just fallen out of bed, hastily dressed in an old T-shirt and jeans. As his eyes fell on Jessica, his face turned pale. 'What the hell are you doing here?' he muttered at her angrily.

Jessica was still reeling from the impact of what the woman in the plastic apron had just said to her. She gaped at her. 'What did you say?' she asked.

'You heard me all right.' The woman gave a derisive laugh. 'This here's my beloved husband. And I'm his beloved wife.' She turned to Graham. 'Isn't that right?'

'Wife?' Jessica looked from one to the other in ashen-faced bewilderment. 'Graham, what's going on here? What's she talking about?' Somehow her brain just couldn't absorb the story that her eyes and ears were telling her.

The woman cut in again before Graham could say a word. 'Don't be so surprised, you're not the first poor innocent he's taken in. But his name's not Graham, my dear. It's Brian. Brian Pierce. And I'm Mrs Pierce. Have been for the past four years.'

Jessica swallowed, feeling a sudden nausea rise in her throat, and her knuckles were white as she clutched for support at the arms of the chair. Never for one moment had she expected to hear anything like this. 'Say something, Graham,' she pleaded in a small voice.

He was watching her without a shred of contrition in his pale blue eyes. 'If you don't want to hear things you'd rather not know, you shouldn't go sticking your nose where it's not wanted,' he said. 'Nobody asked you to come here.'

It was as though he had struck her. Jessica tried to stand up, but she couldn't move. 'Good God, Graham, what's going on? Who are you?' She was talking to a stranger. 'What sort of game have you been playing with me?'

The woman who called herself Mrs Pierce laughed out loud at that. 'What sort of game do you think, you little fool? He was out to get his hands on your precious business, of course! Brian's always been one for short-cuts, you see. Doesn't believe in putting in too much effort himself.' Her small eyes narrowed vindictively. 'That's all you were to him—a short-cut. Make no mistake.' And she cast a proprietorial glance across at her husband now. 'That's all any of them ever are. He always comes back to me in the end.'

Jessica felt as though, at any moment, she might be sick. So this was why he had spent so many weekends away. Why he had always been so cagey about his past. And why he had never seriously attempted to make love to her. Though for this last, at least, she was grateful. If nothing else, she'd been spared the indignity of a squalid affair with a married man. Yet, all at once, she hated him in spite of that.

Slowly, shaking with anger, she somehow managed to rise to her feet. 'You liar! You cheat! You absolute bastard!' And her eyes were filled with hurt and loathing as she went on, 'I should have listened long ago to what Luke Hartt told me about you. He warned me what sort of despicable character you are—but I refused to believe it.' She shook her head. 'You're right, Mrs Pierce, I am a fool.' And fixed her green eyes on Graham again, for the first time seeing him as he really was and fighting to control the cold revulsion he instilled in her. How could she ever have been taken in? And how could she have ever believed that she was in love with him?

With an effort, she straightened, confronting him. 'I know all about you—about all the innocent, defenceless people you've cheated. And I know why Luke Hartt was after you. He told me the story of what you did to his parents' housekeeper.' And she knew now it was true. And everything else that he had told her, too.

Graham didn't try to deny it. Instead, his lips curled contemptuously as he spat at her, 'It sounds like Hartt's been telling you quite a lot! Well, don't bother wasting sympathy on that silly bitch of a housekeeper. She was begging to be fleeced. If I hadn't come along, somebody else would have. She was asking for it!'

'You're despicable!' Disgust and outrage were railing at him from her eyes. 'But you're not going to get away with cheating me. I want you to hand over every penny of the money that you stole from me.'

'Go whistle for it!' He straightened his shoulders aggressively. 'I'm a partner, remember? Half of it's mine by rights, anyway.' His mouth twisted sullenly as he spoke. 'And I'm keeping the lot. I think I'm entitled to a bit of severance pay.'

It was all that Jessica could do to look at him. He was even more contemptible than Hartt had said. 'My partner? Is that what you claim to be? Well, allow me to remind you you've still to pay me for your share of the business!'

'Try and make me! That pathetic agreement we made isn't worth the paper it's written on, and you know it!'

He was right. In a fit of misplaced generosity and trust, Jessica had signed away fifty per cent of her business on little more than a handshake and a promise from him. A promise, she realised now, he had never intended to keep. And she didn't have a leg to stand on legally.

'You bastard!' She hissed the word like poison at him. 'You reptile! I'm getting out of here. You disgust me!' And on shaky legs, she stumbled towards the door, pausing only to deliver one final rebuke at Mrs Pierce. 'Believe me, you're more than welcome to him! I wouldn't have him if he were the very last man on earth!'

Then she was heading, as fast as her legs would carry her, back down the hall, out through the front door and headlong down the path. Surely this couldn't really be happening to her? It was a nightmare. Any minute, she'd wake up. She flung the gate wide—blind to the road ahead of her—and slammed straight into the tall, dark figure who was waiting there.

'Jessica, are you all right?'

Her eyes jerked upwards to meet Hartt's, surprise and an odd sense of relief rushing through her at the sight of him. 'Perfectly,' she somehow managed to affirm, though the muscles of her face felt too stiff, too frozen, to attempt an accompanying smile.

'Well, you don't look it.' Luke took her arm and started to propel her along the street as though she were a weightless, helpless doll. 'I should never have allowed you to go in there. Damn Cole!' And he pulled open the door of the waiting car. 'Let's get the hell out of here before I go back and break his neck!' And he lifted her almost bodily inside.

She fell back into the deep, soft seat and just sat there, as lifeless and immobile as a puppet without strings. She felt as though she'd been pole-axed, every last gasp of energy knocked out of her, both physically and mentally. And she breathed in deep to fight back the tears that suddenly welled up in her eyes. Let Hartt not see this ultimate foolishness, the helpless confusion, the bitter betrayal that she felt. Let her not add to her shame by breaking down in front of him.

He climbed in beside her and she could feel the dark eyes on her face. 'From the look of you, I'd say that the last thing you need now is a long journey south.' He started the engine up. 'We'll go back to the hotel and give you a chance to sort yourself out.'

She nodded dumbly. Just so long as she didn't have to make any decisions for herself right now.

'We can stay another night at the same place. I think that's best. There's no particular hurry for either of us to get back.'

Jessica swallowed, still fighting to control herself. She had half expected him to say, 'I told you so.' And, in a way, she almost wished he had. It would have been easier to cope with than this unexpected display of concern. Criticism and abuse, after all, seemed to be the order of the day. And she bit down fiercely on her lip, as the lump in her throat almost threatened to explode. 'That's fine by me,' she told him in a shaky voice.

They were out of Warley now and heading for the ring road round Birmingham. But the grey eyes never seemed to leave her face. 'Jessica, I'm sorry this had to happen.' Quite unexpectly, he reached out his hand. 'I would have done almost anything to have prevented it.'

She wanted to push his hand away as it covered hers. At the same time, she wanted more than anything to hold on to it. But somehow she could do neither. It was as though she was suddenly paralysed. 'It's my own fault,' she answered, only dimly aware that her limbs were trembling. 'I should have listened to you. I should have had the sense to see it for myself.'

'No, Jessica. Don't blame yourself. Whatever you do, you mustn't do that.' Then, as she dropped her head and refused to look at him, in a single movement he pulled over to the side of the road and reached out to draw her protectively into his arms.

It was almost more than she could bear. With a sob, she let her face fall on his chest and gave release at last to the flood of bitter tears that she'd been holding back. And as he held her there, his fingers gently stroking her hair, his arms enveloping her in their strength, it almost seemed as though he could shield her for ever from all the hurts and harm of life.

'It's all right, Jessica. I promise. Everything's going to be all right.'

And though, deep in her heart, she somehow doubted that—it would be a long, long time before anything was all right again—she felt deeply grateful for the calm, confronting presence of him. She buried her face against his chest and cried till there were no more tears inside her left to cry.

They were re-allocated the rooms they'd occupied previously at the hotel. As the bell-boy ac-

companied them first to Jessica's and deposited her
bag, Luke handed him a bill and bade him leave
them alone.

The boy nodded politely. 'Here are your keys,
sir. I'll take your bag along to the other room.'

As the door closed, Luke crossed to the fridge-
bar and extracted two miniatures of brandy, poured
them and handed one to Jessica. 'Drink this,' he
commanded. 'It'll do you good.'

She seated herself in one of the armchairs that
were arranged round a small coffee-table at the
window end of the room and smiled wanly at him.
The situation was ironically reminiscent of that first
time she had gone to see him at the Old Mill House.
He had offered her a medicinal brandy then as well.
Only this time, she had a great deal more to recover
from than almost falling off a horse. She took a
mouthful. 'Thank you,' she said.

He sat down opposite her. 'How are you feeling
now?'

'Much better.' Still slightly shaky and numb
inside, but nothing like as shattered as she'd felt
less than an hour ago.

Hartt leaned forward in his seat, with that darkly
intent look in his eyes that she had come to know.
'I'm really sorry you had to go through this,' he
told her. 'I take it the wife was present when you
called?'

Jessica nodded. 'Very much so, I'm afraid.'

He shook his head in a gesture of mingled sorrow
and contempt. 'That was unfortunate. Meeting her
face to face can't have been the most pleasant of
experiences.' He sighed and glanced down for a
moment into his glass. 'I would have told you about

her myself, only I didn't know until yesterday that she was still on the scene. I'd been informed, mistakenly, that the woman he was keeping in Warley was just another of his bits on the side.'

Though she knew he had not meant to offend her, Jessica winced at his choice of words. 'He's had quite a number, I understand.'

'I'm sorry.' He paused and scrutinised her face. 'But there was another reason I didn't tell you about his wife.' And for a moment, a hint of the old malice seemed to flit across the dark-tanned face. 'I knew you wouldn't believe me. You never believe anything I say. So I decided it wouldn't be a bad idea if you were forced to face the evidence of your own eyes.' Then his features softened again as he added, 'That was why I insisted on coming along. I didn't want you to face it alone. And I also wanted one last shot at changing your mind.'

'Well, you certainly tried.' She shook her head self-deprecatingly. 'It's not your fault if I'm pigheaded as well as blind.'

He leaned back in his seat and frowned earnestly across at her. 'You know, you really shouldn't be too hard on yourself, Jessica. Cole's a lying, cheating bastard, and what he's done to you is no less than despicable. But, remember, the man's a master of deception. That's how he's made his living for years. He's taken in hundreds, if not thousands, of innocent people in his time, and I've no doubt he really pulled out all the stops with you. Probably most people would have been taken in if they'd been in your shoes.'

Perhaps he was right. But she still felt slightly ashamed of how totally gullible she'd been. 'I didn't even know his name. His real name, I mean. Pierce. Brian Pierce, that's what he's really called—not Graham Cole at all.'

'Pierce? Cole? What's the difference? When you've gone under as many aliases as he has, names don't matter much any more.' And he leaned forward suddenly and fixed his dark eyes on her face. 'The important thing now is that you put him and this entire episode out of your mind. For God's sake, don't let that bastard break your heart. He's not worth it. Put it all behind you. Make a fresh start.'

Easy to say from where he was sitting! He hadn't just witnessed his entire world reduced to bitter ashes at his feet. But Jessica recognised the wisdom in his advice. She took a deep breath and stared down at the carpet. 'In a way, I'm almost glad that it turned out he had a wife. Any feelings I ever imagined I had for him were killed stone-dead the moment I discovered that.' And it was absolutely true. She felt nothing for Graham any more. Just a deep sense of betrayal and a bitter contempt.

'I'm glad to hear it, Jessica.' He smiled. 'That part of your life is over. Just be grateful and start looking forward to what's ahead.'

But what was there to look forward to? For one thing, all her money was gone. For another, along with her belief in Graham, something more important had died—her belief in herself. She'd been so wrong about so many things. How could she trust her own judgement ever again?

She drained her glass and smiled brightly across at Hartt. The future was something she would face in good time. For now, all she really wanted was just to forget. 'I think I'd like another one of these,' she told him, holding out her empty glass. The first had had a pleasantly anaesthetic effect.

'I don't think so.' He took the glass from her hand and laid it, very pointedly, to one side. 'Getting drunk isn't going to do you any good, you know.'

She gave a scoffing little laugh. 'On the contrary, I think it would do me a great deal of good. Can you think of a better way to make me stop feeling what a fool I've been?'

Hartt gave her a long look and said nothing for a moment or two. Then he suggested, 'Perhaps I ought to leave you now.' He started to rise slowly to his feet. 'Maybe you'd like to be left on your own for a while.'

But she didn't want him to go, and she didn't want to be left on her own. 'I wouldn't. Really,' she started to protest, but already he was starting to move past her, towards the door.

'I think you ought to try and have a rest,' he said.

She stood up abruptly in front of him. 'I'm not tired.' Why was he suddenly in such a hurry to leave? And she lifted her gaze questioningly to his face—and in that same instant saw her answer burning in his eyes.

'Luke?'

For the briefest of seconds, the dark eyes seemed to bore down to her very soul, then his hand reached out to cup her chin tilting her face upwards towards his. And it seemed as though the world stood still as he bent down at last to cover her lips with his, gently, almost tentatively at first, as though he might still draw away from her. Then, as his arms went round her, pulling her close to him, she could feel the burning pressure of his mouth increase, fierce and demanding, as he persuaded her own eager lips to part and flicked his tongue lightly against her teeth, exploring the inner sweetness of her mouth.

This time, she did not resist. As his body pressed against her, hard and strong, and she could feel the desire rising in him, she closed her eyes and allowed the spark of passion that glowed within her own flesh to ignite. With a sigh, she slid her arms around his neck, letting her fingers ripple through the thick, dark hair, caressing the warm and supple softness at the back of his neck and letting her hand slide down inside the open collar of his shirt to touch the smooth-muscled flesh of his shoulders and back.

It was delicious, this sensation of fire licking against her skin, as his lips ran a trail of kisses along the line of her jaw and throat and his hand reached up to cup her breast, his palm moulding to contain its roundness as his thumb stroked at her nipple through the thin cotton of her blouse. She could feel his breathing, rough and ragged against her face, and her own heart beating wildly inside her chest as he raised his head and whispered against her ear, 'Jessica, I want to make love to you.'

'Oh, yes!' It was as much a cry of supplication as assent. She wanted him at that moment more than anything. And her legs felt suddenly nerveless as he took her by the hand and led her silently towards the bed.

The coverlet was cool against her back, his fingers warm as he leaned over her and started to undo the buttons of her blouse. And she could feel the blood thundering in her veins as his mouth closed over hers again, hungry and hard, and she felt him pull her blouse away to expose her naked, excited breasts.

'Oh, Jessica, you're beautiful!' And she gasped out loud as he stooped to take their fullness firmly with both hands, then dropped his head to claim with his lips each aching rosy peak in turn.

'Luke, there's something I ought to tell you.' Her hands were in his hair as he slid away her skirt and briefs and paused to gaze down on her naked loveliness. Then the burgundy-coloured shirt fell to the floor and a moment later he was naked beside her, the long, bronzed length of him pressed urgently against her hips and thighs, as the dark eyes lingered for a moment on her face.

'I know, Jessica. This is your first time, isn't it?'

She nodded and reached out to touch the smooth dark shoulders and delicately stroke the magnificent, hair-roughened chest, unsure, really, why she'd wanted him to know.

But he seemed to understand. 'Don't worry, Jessica,' he was saying as his hand lightly caressed her breast. 'You're mine now. And that's what you were always meant to be.'

His lovemaking was beautiful. Sensitive and gentle and passionate and wild. He seemed to know instinctively what her senses craved, as his lips and hands moved like silk across her body, coaxing and caressing to a pitch of arousal so intense that it was almost pain.

No more! her flesh was calling, as she felt his hand slide down to ease her aching thighs apart. Her back arched, begging for the ultimate consummation, as his weight crushed down on her. Then she felt the breath leave her body as, at last, in one sharp, thrusting movement, he became a part of her.

It was the sweetest of pains, brief and exquisite, then her body seemed to be filled with an intensity of sensations that was at once within her and all around her, carrying her helplessly towards some peak that she had never climbed before.

She came to suddenly, half believing it had been a dream.

'You dozed off.' He was seated on the edge of the bed, a towel tied loosely around his waist, his dark hair wet and glistening from the shower.

Jessica felt herself blush at the sight of him. The last thing she remembered, in the lazy aftermath of love, was curling up in his arms with a feeling of total contentment and peace. And wishing, just before she must have drifted off, that the moment would never end.

He leaned to kiss her. 'How do you feel?'

'OK.' Suddenly awkward, she pulled herself up against the pillows and snatched the rumpled sheet to her breasts, to hide her nakedness from him.

He smiled. 'Too late for that now, Jessica. We have no secrets from each other any more.' And, as her blush grew deeper, he reached out a hand to caress her shoulders and neck. 'No regrets, I hope?' he asked.

Oh, no! She regretted nothing. Just then, he had given her the sweetest moments of her life. She shook her head. 'Of course not,' she assured him. 'I wanted it as much as you.' And blushed again at her own boldness. 'I don't regret it a bit.'

'Good.' He reached out and took hold of her hand. 'That's what I was hoping to hear.' And, in a gesture that was pure Gallic in its spontaneous charm, he lifted her fingers lightly to his lips and smiled across at her with those splendid dark eyes. 'And what I hope always to hear from you.'

She smiled at him gratefully. He had transformed this day of horrors into one that would remain for ever special in her memory.

'And now I have a suggestion to make,' he went on in a more practical vein. 'I don't know about you, but I'm starving. I suggest we phone down to room service and order something. Then, if you're willing, we can drive into Birmingham and take a look around. It's not exactly a beautiful city, but there's plenty to see. And we can keep an eye open for some place interesting to have dinner tonight.'

Jessica laughed. So he had it all planned, virtually down to the last detail! But for once the arrangements suited her perfectly. She was in no hurry to leave this place nor to get down to the painful business of piecing together the shattered fragments of her life. This brief interlude, she felt, was exactly what she required. A welcome and thoroughly therapeutic break from harsh reality. And perhaps Luke understood that, too. 'You're in charge,' she told him, delivering a playful dig in the ribs. 'Just for a change, you're not going to hear a single argument from me.'

'And about time, too.' And he tried to catch hold of her as she slid from the bed, dragging the long sheet behind her like a veil of modesty as she went. But she was too quick for him, as she darted on nimble legs towards the bathroom door.

'But don't think I'm going soft,' she advised him over her shoulder. 'I'll be looking out for my own interests a little more seriously from now on.'

He caught the sheet by a corner and forced her to pause and look round at him, and his expression was suddenly serious again. 'Don't worry, Jessica,' he told her. 'No one's ever going to hurt you again. I won't let them. You have my solemn promise on that.'

It was an odd sort of promise to make, she thought as she sank into a bubble bath and listened to him making the room service order over the phone. Touching in its kindness, though she knew better than to take it seriously. He was simply trying to reassure her, to help restore her shattered confidence after her awful shock. For, contrary to what she'd first believed of him, she knew now that Luke Hartt was a deeply compassionate man. A decent man, behind the ruthless mask he sometimes liked to wear; the sort of man it would be far too easy to rely upon. And relying on him—or on any other man—was something she must never, ever do again.

The hours spent with Luke that day she would remember for ever as magical. They did nothing in particular—visited an art gallery or two, drank coffee, toured the historic buildings—and laughed a lot. And Jessica found herself wishing that she'd got to know this humorous, light-hearted side of him much earlier. What a shameful waste all that time of bitter antagonism had been! What a lot of bad blood they'd built up between them, when all the time they could have been friends.

She watched him through lowered lashes as he ordered dinner for them that evening in the little Italian restaurant that she'd picked out, and she was suddenly filled with a sense of regret. Today, the day the two of them had finally decided to drop hostilities and come together in harmony, was probably the only day they'd ever have. Tomorrow, back in the real world, fate would set them once more on their separate paths.

The waiter brought *conchiglie alla romana* and poured the wine. 'I'll say one thing,' Jessica admitted with a smile, as she set about demolishing the plateful of creamy, garlicky pasta shells. 'I've never eaten better in my life than I have over the past few days.'

He returned her smile. 'And I've never enjoyed such stimulating company. You're quite a girl, Jessica. I've never met anyone like you before.'

She made a face and teased him, though she was really flattered by the compliment. 'Not even in any of your previous lives?'

He laughed, remembering the remark he'd made at the dinner party the other night. Was that really only two days ago? So much had happened, so much had changed! 'No, not in any of them, I'm afraid. I always seem to meet the wrong type of girl. The type who's after my money, or just simply out for a good time.' And he smiled a wry smile. 'Not much luck in that department to date, I'm afraid. Much like yourself.' Then he added, his tone suddenly sober, 'I wish to God I'd met you before that bastard Cole came along. Things would have been very different.'

'Maybe.' Abruptly, Jessica dropped her eyes, oddly discomfited by the sudden dark frown between his brows and by the way the conversation had so unexpectedly shifted to the subject of Graham. She'd been hoping to avoid that particular topic, at least tonight.

But Luke evidently intended otherwise. 'Tomorrow I'll make an appointment for you to see my lawyer,' he was saying. 'He's the best there is. He'll advise you as to what legal action you should take.'

Jessica shook her head, adamant. 'No!' Then went on quickly before he could insist, 'I'm not ready to start thinking about that. Please, let's just leave it for now. I have to get my mind straight first.'

He sat back in his seat and sighed. 'OK.' Though she could sense the reluctance in him. 'But you can't put it to one side indefinitely, Jessica. He stole your money. You can't let him get away with that.'

'I know, I know. I just need time. Please, Luke, try to understand.'

He reached across the table and clasped her hand. 'OK, Jessica. I'll wait for you to say the word.'

With that, thankfully, the subject was dropped, and Jessica settled back to enjoy the rest of the evening. Much like a condemned man making the most of his last moments, she thought. There would be time enough to face all the unpleasantness later. But, for the brief period that remained to her, she just wanted to put it all from her mind.

As they drove back to the hotel, she was feeling positively light-hearted, laughing happily at Luke's jokes. They walked across the lobby arm in arm, as though they'd been friends and lovers for years, and collected their keys at the reception desk. Then, as they headed towards the lift, he suddenly paused and grinned down at her, 'Your place or mine for a nightcap?' he wanted to know.

She barely hesitated. 'Yours.' What was the point in pretending? She didn't want to let him go. Not yet.

It was a night to crown the shared precious hours that had preceded it. A night that was perfect, like a dream. As he came to her, his naked body cool against hers at first, she felt the thrill that only his touch could provoke and pressed herself into his arms, eager to receive him and to give herself.

It was even more perfect than before, his lips, his hands, seeming to trigger responses from her that were ever more instantaneous and ever more intense. And as he gently guided her, she learned how to reciprocate the pleasure that he gave to her, her senses revelling in the velvet-soft touch of him, desire knifing through her like a lance as she felt the hardness of his thighs bear down on hers and the rough scrape of his chest against her breasts. Then she cried out as the frenzy finally unleashed itself and she felt herself plummet from the sky into a sweet and timeless void.

He was lying with his face towards her, one hand lightly across her breast, and she could tell from his slow and easy breathing that he was fast asleep. She had lain there, quite still, beside him for the past couple of hours, listening and watching as the dark silhouette of his head grew gradually clearer in the soft, filtering glow of dawn. And she sighed now, almost regretfully, and stirred. It was time.

Soft as a feather, Jessica gently slid his hand away, then eased herself slowly from the bed and crossed the room to tiptoe to the chair where she had left her clothes. She held her breath anxiously as, for a moment, the sleeping figure seemed to stir. Then she breathed with relief, hastily fumbling with the buttons of her blouse, as he sighed and rolled over on to his other side and the peaceful, rhythmic breathing gradually resumed.

She crossed to where her bag and her room key lay, and picked them up, careful not to make a sound. Then she hurried over to the door and, with only the briefest of backward glances at the figure sleeping in the bed, slipped out into the corridor.

The next moment, she was racing as fast as her legs would carry her towards her room, her heart beating fearfully inside her breast as she fumbled briefly with the lock before stumbling inside. She went straight to the phone. 'Get me a taxi. Right away.'

It took her less than a minute to pack. She simply threw her few things into the overnight bag. Then she was hurrying back down the empty corridor towards the lift, a firm, if fearful, resolve in her step and a prayer for the future in her heart. It was five-thirty on an August morning and Jessica was taking the only dignified course of action that seemed open to her now. She was leaving. Turning her back on all of it. The pain. The past. And all the mistakes she had made.

And saying goodbye for ever to Luke.

CHAPTER EIGHT

'JESSICA! How many times must I tell you not to do that?!' Sid Edelman came bustling up to his young assistant, the kind eyes behind the thick-lensed spectacles full of concern, the bald head shaking disapprovingly at her as she attempted to shift a large, half-empty crate across the storeroom floor. 'You shouldn't be doing that sort of thing. Why didn't you call through for me?'

'I can manage.' Jessica straightened and smiled at him. 'I just wanted to get this out of the way before the next delivery arrives.' The effort, however, had brought a sudden dizzying rush of blood to her head. Mr Edelman was probably right.

He came up to her, forefinger waggling in ad-monishment. 'You go through and attend to the customers,' he told her. 'That's what I employ a pretty young woman like you for—not for heaving heavy crates of furniture about.'

Jessica threw an affectionate glance at the small, portly figure who had been so good to her over the past few months. 'You're the boss,' she conceded with a good-natured shrug.

'And don't you forget it!' He waved a fist jok-ingly at her. 'Now off you go, young lady, and sell some merchandise for me.'

Jessica smiled to herself as she hurried through to the front of the shop. For all his light-hearted attempts to bully her, he was one of the kindest-hearted men she'd ever known. If it hadn't been for Sid Edelman, Jessica seriously doubted that she could have got through the past three and a half months still in one piece. He'd been almost like a father to her during the loneliest, most deeply unhappy period of her entire life.

A handful of customers were browsing around the shelves. Even at this time of the year—nearly December—there were still quite a few tourists about in London, and a surprising number of them managed to stray as far afield as Sid Edelman's antiques shop in darkest Fulham. But, amid the plaid jackets and Crimplene trews, there was one particular customer who caught Jessica's eye. A woman standing with her back to her. A short figure in a big tweed coat, with an unbecoming green woollen beret pulled down over her ears. Jessica had noticed her earlier in the afternoon, hovering outside in the street and peering through the shop window from time to time, as though she had something other than simply shopping for antiques on her mind.

Very deliberately, Jessica walked up to her now. 'May I help you?' she asked.

The woman swung round nervously, her eyes squinting short-sightedly from her thin, pale face. 'No, thank you. I'm just looking,' she said. And, as she started to edge away towards the door, it struck Jessica, as it had before, that there was something faintly familiar about her. But, before she could figure out what it was, she was interrupted by a Texan drawl.

'Excuse me, miss. Could you just explain to us what this here object's for?' And, as she turned to attend to the query, the woman in the woollen beret slipped quietly out of the door.

But she was still very much on Jessica's mind that evening as she left the shop. Waving goodbye to Mr Edelman, she turned up the collar of her thin coat against the biting November wind as she set out on her regular two-mile hike home. Maybe it was her over-wrought imagination playing tricks on her, or maybe she really did catch a glimpse of the green-bereted woman just as she was sticking her front-door key in the lock—but, in any case, she closed the door sharply behind her and literally sprinted up the shabby staircase to the room she rented at the top.

Who was the woman? What did she want with her? And she felt a sharp stab of apprehension at the thought that she might possibly be following her. Could it be that someone from her past was trying to track her down? Jessica shivered and leaned her back against the door with a sigh. Would she have to keep running for ever? Was there really no escape?

She lit the gas fire and put the kettle on the stove, then paused for a moment to gaze wistfully out of the window at the darkened skyline. For, off in the distance, rising like a ship's proud mast above the untidy clutter of roofs, she could just make out the outline of the Minerva tower. And that was really why she had taken this room—though she knew it was madness to spend her evenings gazing sadly out at it, watching the lights she could sometimes see blazing late into the night, imagining him still at work on the fifteenth floor or relaxing in his penthouse suite. Luke Hartt was the very last person she should be thinking of. Hadn't he been the final straw that had triggered her lonely flight?

Since that morning, that seemed now like a lifetime ago, when she had fled from their hotel in Birmingham, leaving Luke still sleeping unawares in the bed they had so briefly shared, she had neither seen him nor been in touch with him—nor had she ever been back to Harbingdon.

She'd phoned Deirdre a couple of days later, just to let her know that she was safe.

'Thank God you've phoned! I've been nearly out of my mind!'

She'd felt a pang of conscience at the undisguised concern in Deirdre's voice. 'Well, you can stop worrying,' she'd told her. 'I'm all right.'

'Where are you, Jessica? What's going on?'

But Jessica was determined to give nothing away. 'Don't worry about me,' she hedged. 'I promise you there's nothing to be concerned about.'

'I'm glad to hear it.' Deirdre paused. 'And I know someone else who'll be glad, too. Luke Hartt. He's been scouring the countryside for you for the past two days.'

An anxious warning bell had sounded in Jessica's heart. The last person in the world she wanted to find her now was Luke. 'Well, you can tell him to call off the search. I don't want him making a fuss.'

'I'll tell him. But you tell me something—when are you coming home?'

'I'm not.' She'd spoken the words quickly, trying to hide how much it hurt her to utter them as she went on, 'I've got myself a job and a place to live. I'm never coming back to Harbingdon.'

'But that's ridiculous! Jessica, this is your home!'

'Not any more.' Her hands were suddenly trembling, her voice thick. 'I can't come back. Try to understand, Deirdre.' And she'd slammed the phone down quickly before her friend could try to change her mind.

The next day, without revealing where she was, she'd contacted her solicitor in Kent, instructing him to wind up Bridge Antiques and sell the flat, then use the proceeds to settle any outstanding debts and pay Deirdre a generous redundancy settlement. Anything that was left was to be paid into her Harbingdon bank account, and from there transferred anonymously to a new account in London. She'd been surprised and pleased, both at the speed of the transaction and at the amount, when a few weeks later a sum of several thousand pounds had been credited. After what she'd read in the newspapers about Graham's debts, she'd been expecting a great deal less.

It had been just two weeks after she'd seen him in Warley that Graham had been arrested, on a number of charges of fraud and deception, according to the report she'd read. And, from the weight of evidence ranged against him, it looked as though most of the charges would stick. Graham, it seemed almost certain now, was destined to spend a fairly lengthy spell in jail.

Jessica had felt nothing when she'd read that. Neither sorrow nor pleasure, just a vague sense of regret. Belatedly, she realised how little he'd ever really meant to her. What she'd once thought was love had been nothing more than mild affection—and even that had been based on a lie. Love, she knew now, was not that gentle, almost passive, emotion that she'd felt for Graham. It was a fierce and all-consuming passion that filled the heart with joy and anguish and could tear apart your very soul.

She poured herself a cup of tea and sat down with a defeated sigh. Trust her to choose the wrong man to teach her about love. Trust her to give her heart—almost without realising that it was happening—to a man whom, quite simply, she could never have. And she raised her eyes to the window with regret and swallowed back the tearful lump that had risen in her throat. He had shown kindness to her in her hour of need, and she would always be grateful to him for that. But even in her state of semi-shock that day, she'd sensed the danger she was in. Graham had bruised her pride and shaken her faith in herself and human nature temporarily—but Luke Hartt was capable of a great deal worse. He'd break her heart if she let him. And that was really the reason why she'd run away. Though she hadn't known then, of course, of the bitter-sweet legacy of their one day of love that she carried with her.

She sighed again and pulled the dingy curtains shut. That was her secret. The one good thing to come out of this mess. At least she would always have a part of him.

It was one morning a couple of days later, when things were quiet at the shop, that Mr Edelman suggested to her, 'Let's have one of our special elevenses. You nip along to the delicatessen for a couple of bagels and I'll make a pot of coffee.'

'Good idea.' Jessica smiled at him. Treats like bagels were something she had to rely on Mr

Edelman for these days. Her salary covered only the bare essentials, and though she had a bit of money in the bank she hadn't touched a penny of it. That was for the baby when it came.

She pulled on her coat and hurried outside, heading briskly for the little corner shop a couple of blocks away and, for the umpteenth time, congratulating herself on having found herself such a kind-hearted boss. When she'd told him about the baby—and he was the only person she *had* told—he'd assured her she could stay on at the shop for as long as she felt able, and that her job would be waiting for her whenever she wanted to come back. How could she ever manage without him? she wondered now.

She was so preoccupied with these thoughts as she emerged from the delicatessen that she almost didn't notice the woman in the green beret who was hovering in a doorway across the street. But, as the woman stepped forward, Jessica glanced up suddenly and caught sight of her, her heart turning over in panic as, in the very same instant, she saw the car. A sinister, dark shadow parked up a side street and moving slowly towards her now. And she could feel her heart pounding against her ribs and her breath catch painfully, deep in her chest, as she turned and raced off blindly the other way, running as fast as fast as her legs would carry her.

But they could not carry her fast enough. From the corner of her eye, she could see the dark blue shadow gaining on her. Then there was a sharp squeal of brakes, a quick shuffle of footsteps and she felt a strong hand grab her by the arm.

'Let me go! Let me go!' she tried to scream.

But she was already being bundled into the back seat of the warm, leather-scented Rolls. And the fingers of the hand clamped round her arm were like a vice as Hartt pushed her back against the seat and indicated to the chauffeur to drive on. 'Oh no, Jessica,' he growled. 'You're not running away from me a second time!'

Jessica fell back, limp and breathless, and did not dare to look at him at first. 'What the hell do you think you're doing?' she demanded. 'What do you want with me?'

'What I'd like to do with you right now is strangle you,' he informed her harshly. 'And I reckon it would be no more than you deserve.'

Her eyes snapped open then and she spun round, in alarm, to look at him. 'And what is that supposed to mean?'

In spite of herself, she felt a helpless thrill of pleasure at the sight of him, though her heart contracted at the way his face appeared thinner, more pinched somehow, with visible lines of tension around the eyes and mouth. It looked as though the past fourteen weeks had been almost as hard on him as they'd been on her.

The expression in the dark grey eyes was grave as they met hers. 'Save your breath for *answering* questions,' he advised her in a steely tone. 'I'm the one who's going to be doing the asking around here, not you.'

She struggled feebly against the hand still fastened around her arm, pinning her against the seat—almost as though he feared she might try to hurl herself out of the car. 'Where are you taking me?' she wanted to know.

The dark eyes flicked across impatiently at her. 'To somewhere private—where we can talk.'

She threw him a sarcastic look and tried to smother the sudden stab of apprehension that she felt. 'And what about Miss Clutton? Are you just going to leave her behind—after her doing such a diligent job of tracking me down?'

A brief, weary smile flitted across his handsome face. 'Yes, she did do rather a good job, didn't she? Though I knew it wouldn't take you long to see through her disguise.' He paused. 'But you really needn't concern yourself about Miss Clutton, you know. As I've already told you, she'll be handsomely rewarded for her pains—and I'm sure she's perfectly capable of finding her own way home.' Then he sat back in his seat and fixed her with those penetrating eyes. 'Besides, you and I have much more urgent matters than Miss Clutton to discuss.'

Jessica turned and looked out of the window as his words sent an anxious chill through her. What did he mean? Was it possible that he was about to bring even more disaster down upon her head?

They were heading for the Minerva building. Jessica felt her heart sink as they swept down into the underground car park and Luke assisted her out of the car. So the confrontation was to be on his home ground. And she felt the tension in her rise almost to screaming point as he led her into the lift and pressed the button for the penthouse suite. She was being carried off to his private eyrie like the helpless victim of some bird of prey.

Then they were stepping into an enormous hall, and from there into a huge reception room illuminated by the pale November light that streamed in through the window along one wall.

Luke stripped off his jacket and flung it into the corner of one of the tan leather-upholstered sofas. Then strode swiftly over to the bar. 'I need a brandy,' he told her. 'How about you?'

Jessica remained standing awkwardly in the middle of the room, her fists thrust deep into the pockets of her thin coat. 'No, thank you. I won't have any.' She'd resolved to stay off spirits for the duration of her pregnancy.

'Suit yourself.' He poured himself a stiff measure and downed it in one gulp. Replenishing his glass, he crossed to one of the matching leather arm-chairs facing her and dropped his long frame into it. 'And now I'd like to hear some explanations from you.'

His tone was imperious, commanding, but it struck Jessica that he was no longer quite the cool, totally self-possessed Luke Hartt she had once known. There was a shadow, almost of doubt, in the dark eyes, as he added more softly, 'Why did you do it, Jessica? What made you pull that disappearing act?'

She took a deep breath. 'I had to. There was nothing for me to stay for any more.' She pulled her coat more tightly about her. 'I just didn't have the heart to go on with my old life any more.'

'Because of Cole? Surely not. Don't tell me that bastard really did break your heart, after all?'

'Of course not.' She shook her head. How could she possibly tell him the truth? 'I had my reasons. That's really all you need to know.'

He shot her a disapproving look. 'So you turned your back on everything, just like that! Do you think that was a good thing to do? Just walk out on all your responsibilities?'

So he had brought her here just to cast up her supposed misdeeds. 'It was the best I could do in the circumstances,' she shot back at him angrily. 'I'm sure Deirdre had no difficulty in finding another job.'

'Did you ever bother to find out?' Then he added, before she could say anything, 'No, of course you didn't. You didn't give a damn for Deirdre or for anyone else. The only person you were thinking of was yourself!'

'That isn't fair!' And it wasn't—though she had felt a twinge of guilt over her friend more than once during the past few months. She forced herself to meet his eyes. 'Since you seem to know so much— *did* she manage to find another job?'

He sat back impatiently in his seat and drank back the brandy before answering. 'In the event, she didn't need to,' he said.

Jessica frowned down at him. 'Didn't need to? What do you mean?'

The dark eyes narrowed, deliberately mysterious. 'Why don't you sit down and take off your coat?' he suggested. 'Isn't it warm enough in here for you?'

With her coat on, it was almost uncomfortably warm, but Jessica felt loath to remove it somehow. Without it, she would feel even more exposed and vulnerable. And she'd be even more totally at his mercy if she sat down. She hugged the coat more tightly about her and stood her ground. 'I asked you what you meant when you said that Deirdre didn't need to find another job.'

He held her eyes for a long moment before answering. 'I mean that she's still working at Bridge Antiques.'

'That isn't possible.' He was playing some kind of game with her. 'The shop's been sold. And the flat. Bridge Antiques doesn't exist any more.'

He shook his head slowly as he continued to look at her. 'No, Jessica, you're wrong. Nothing's been sold. Everything's exactly as you left it—except that the debts Cole left you with have been settled, the business is thriving, and you are the sole owner once again. I had a bit of pressure applied to Cole, just before he was arrested, and he was more than happy to sign his share back to you.'

Jessica's mouth fell open. Was he serious? Could this fairy-tale that he was telling her really be true? 'But what about the money that was paid into my bank account? The money from the sale of the shop and the flat?'

He made a wry face. 'That was my doing, I'm afraid. Once I'd talked your solicitors into taking the property off the market, I realised you'd probably be in need of cash—considering the way you ran off with only the clothes you stood up in to your name. I didn't want you to end up starving on the street, so I arranged for a few thousand pounds to be paid into your account.'

A strange, ambiguous feeling went through her as she listened to him. She dropped her eyes in sudden confusion to the floor. 'You had no right to do that,' she said.

'Right or not, I did it. For once, you weren't around to argue with me.' He shook his head. 'Though, judging from the look of the place you were staying in, you haven't spent very much of it.'

'I couldn't. I was keeping it for the——' Jessica stopped herself just in time, appalled at how close she'd come to revealing her most private secret to him. Then she quickly moved to the attack. 'I suppose we have you to thank for Graham's arrest? No doubt you engineered that as well?'

'I'm afraid not,' he told her with an expression of mock-regret. 'That was the unaided work of the Kent Constabulary.' He threw her an ironic smile. 'I guess it was just finally time for him to pay his dues. I can assure you,' he added, draining his glass, 'I, personally, have no further interest in him.'

She was glad to hear it, though not out of any sense of compassion for Graham. It was just nice to know that Graham no longer figured in either of their lives. She stood for a moment staring at Luke, an odd mix of emotions assailing her. 'Why did you save Bridge Antiques?' she asked.

He took a deep breath. 'I thought it was the least I could do. As I warned you a long time ago, Cole would have left you penniless anyway, but perhaps my contribution to events didn't exactly make things easier for you.' And he smiled a regretful smile. 'But I promise I'm through now with interfering with your life. You can go back to Harbingdon absolutely certain of that. I'm even prepared to sell the Old Mill House and move out of the district completely, so you need never set eyes on me again.'

Abruptly, Jessica turned to the window, her back to him, and stared outside. It was what she'd once thought she wanted, why she'd run away. Yet now his words sent a shiver through her, like icy water dousing her soul. Her eyes were fixed unseeingly on the grey November sky. 'That's very generous of you,' she said.

And it was. What he'd already done and what he was offering were far more than he owed. Yet it was all so tragically wrong. What she truly longed for was something he could never give—his love and the privilege of experiencing for the rest of her days the joy that she'd experienced today when she'd opened her eyes to see his face. It was a cruel irony that he believed he was doing a favour by offering to disappear for ever from her life.

She heard a sharp intake of breath. 'Generosity has nothing to do with it.' Then a slight movement as he rose to his feet. And she felt her shoulders stiffen defensively as he came softly across the room towards her and stopped just a few paces away. 'Tell me the truth, Jessica, why did you run away like that? Whatever your problems, surely you knew I'd help?'

Jessica swallowed hard. He was standing far too close, and his nearness and the words he spoke were almost breaking her heart. 'I didn't know anything,' she somehow managed to whisper in reply.

'How can you say that?' Suddenly, his hand was on her shoulder, spinning her round to look at him, and there was an almost ferocious intensity in the grey eyes that burned down into hers. 'After what passed between us that day, how can you say a thing like that?'

She could feel her lips trembling. 'I know you were kind to me that day, but I couldn't expect you to...'

'Kind?' He was staring down at her as though he could not belive his ears. 'What in the name of heaven made you think that I was being *kind*?' His fingers dug into her shoulders as he gripped her. 'Do you think it's kindness that's had me almost out of my mind for the past fourteen weeks, scouring the country from Land's End to John o' Groats, trying to track you down? Do you think it's kindness that's made me lose nearly half a stone and spend most of my nights unable to sleep?' He shook her gently, with something close to desperation in his eyes. 'Surely you don't honestly believe that I made love to you out of *kindness*, do you?' And a wry, self-deprecatory smile flitted across his face. 'Surely all the things that I was trying to express to you that day didn't *feel* like charity?'

She could scarcely breathe. She felt confused, close to tears, and her heart was hammering so hard that it must surely burst. 'No,' she told him, then added miserably, 'I don't know.'

'Oh, Jessica.' Regret flooded into his eyes. 'I would have told you, but I was certain you wouldn't believe me if I did. I thought it would be better to give us both a little more time.'

His tone was earnest, full of urgency, but what was he trying to say to her? She frowned at him, not daring to ask.

'Time for you to get over Cole,' he went on. 'Time to get used to me.' And the fingers on her shoulders were suddenly soft as they slid round her shoulders to caress her hair. 'But surely you guessed. I love you, Jessica. I've loved you from that very first moment I saw you. I know it probably sounds crazy, but it's absolutely true.'

It didn't sound crazy. It sounded like the most magical declaration she could ever hear. 'Oh, Luke!' She shivered as his arms folded round her, drawing her close, and looked up breathlessly into his eyes. 'I was afraid. That's why I ran away.' Then, nervously, she dropped her gaze again, scarcely daring to utter out loud the words she could no longer manage to hold back. 'You see, I love you, too.'

As his lips came down on hers, it felt as though all the good things in the entire universe were suddenly cascading down upon her head. As though all the pain, the tears and the sorrow had never been. And she clung to him, feeling her heart swell with almost unimaginable happiness as he whispered against her face, 'Marry me, Jessica. Please marry me.'

She was sitting in the middle of the bed, surrounded by a mountain of pillows and discarded tissue paper, when he walked into the room, carrying a bottle of champagne and two glasses, with a gift-wrapped parcel tucked under his arm. And though he'd been gone for less than quarter of an hour, she felt her heart quicken with pleasure at the sight of him. She grinned. 'I thought you were going down to collect the post. What's the bottle of champagne for?'

He crossed the room and bent to kiss her. 'We have something to celebrate,' he said.

She laughed. 'Again?' They seemed to have been doing nothing but celebrate for the past two weeks.

He sat down on the edge of the bed and laid the champagne and glasses on the bedside table. 'But first this.' And he handed the gift-wrapped parcel to her. 'It's from Miss Clutton. She had a messenger bring it round.'

Jessica took the parcel from him with a smile and started to undo the wrappings carefully. She'd lost count of the number of wedding presents that had come pouring in—including a coffee service from Deirdre, who was almost overwhelmed as Jessica herself with the outcome of everything, and a silver cakestand from a delighted Mr Edelman. 'In the hope,' as he put it, 'that you don't make a habit of going out for bagels and getting kidnapped on the way home!' But if this one was from Miss Clutton, then it was extra-special.

She smiled as she laid aside the tissue paper to reveal a beautiful lead crystal vase and read the message on the accompanying card: 'Sincere good wishes for your future happiness together. From Cecily Clutton.'

'How lovely!' Jessica exclaimed.

And the wishes, she knew, were indeed sincere. She had misjudged Miss Clutton all along. The woman was not the cold and calculating automaton that Jessica had thought she was. Beneath that rugged exterior beat a heart of gold. Over the past two weeks, she had come to realise why her future husband valued the woman so. Her devotion and loyalty were limitless—though her duties would be restricted to matters of a purely business nature from now on. As she'd confided to Jessica the other day, 'It's your job to look after his personal welfare now. I'm taking a well earned rest.'

Jessica watched him as he lifted the champagne bottle from the table and started to undo the cork, knowing that she would gladly spend the rest of her days looking after him. Not for nothing had she appointed Deirdre manageress of Bridge Antiques. From now on, she'd be devoting most of her energies to the man she loved. She reached out tenderly to touch his face, noting with satisfaction how all the dense, dark shadows had vanished now, and asked him, 'So what are we celebrating this time?'

He threw her a mysterious smile. 'The answer's in my pocket,' he said.

Curious, she slid her hand into the pocket of his navy silk robe and drew out an airmail envelope. 'Who's it from?' she asked, observing the unfamiliar Australian stamp.

He started to ease away the cork. 'I would suggest that the best way to find out the answer to that is to open it up and read it,' he replied.

Jessica glanced at him suspiciously. It couldn't be. But her hands were trembling excitedly all the same as she ripped open the envelope. With Luke, after all, anything was possible. Then her eyes widened with delight as she read the opening lines of the letter inside. 'Luke! My sister and her family are coming over for the wedding! I'm finally going to meet them all!'

As the cork popped, he turned to grin at her in feigned surprise. 'Well, fancy that!' Then laughed as she threw her arms around his neck, spilling the champagne over her satin nightie and the sheets.

'You organised this, didn't you?' Jessica hugged him, loving every inch of him, then sat back with a huge smile as he filled the two glasses and handed her one. 'And you didn't even tell me you'd been in touch with her!'

'I wanted it to be a surprise.' And he touched the rim of his glass against hers. 'Weddings—and especially weddings that happen to coincide with Christmas—are times for families to get together. And yours has been apart quite long enough.' He drank briefly and laid down his glass. 'You know how I feel about families. They should be close— and the bigger they are the better.' And he reached out and laid his hand on the soft rise of her stomach. 'This is just the beginning, my love.'

She caught his hand and held it there, loving the warm feel of it against her flesh. 'You're pleased, aren't you? About the baby, I mean?' Though she didn't really need to ask. The look of sheer joy on his face when she'd given him the news had been worth a thousand words.

He took the champagne glass from her hand and laid it to one side with his own. 'I couldn't be more pleased. About you, about the baby, about us. You don't seem to realise it yet, but you've made me the happiest man alive.' His arms slipped round her as he drew her down on to the bed. 'You're all I've been searching for all my life.' And he bent to softly kiss away her shoulder straps. 'I love you, Jessica. More than you know.'

And as he raised his head to look at her, she gazed back at him with adoration in her eyes and a depth of happiness far beyond description in her heart. In less than a week's time, in a special ceremony at his parents' villa in the South of France, surrounded by all their family and friends, she would be married to this man. Then they would fly off to the sun for what she knew would be an unforgettable honeymoon—and the start of a wonderful life together as man and wife.

'I love you, too, Luke,' she told him. 'I always will.'

As he bent to kiss her, his lips tasted of champagne. The taste of celebration. The taste of love. And as she slid her hands inside his robe, hugging him to her, she smiled happily to herself. This was how it was going to be. A lifetime of love and celebration and happiness.

Coming Next Month

Available in January wherever paperback books are sold, or through Harlequin Reader Service:

In the U.S.
901 Fuhrmann Blvd.
P.O. Box 1397
Buffalo, N.Y. 14240-1397

In Canada
P.O. Box 603
Fort Erie, Ontario
L2A 5X3

Harlequin Historicals

Step into a world of pulsing adventure, gripping emotion and lush sensuality with these evocative love stories penned by today's best-selling authors in the highest romantic tradition. Pursuing their passionate dreams against a backdrop of the past's most colorful and dramatic moments, our vibrant heroines and dashing heroes will make history come alive for you.

Watch for two new Harlequin Historicals each month, available wherever Harlequin books are sold. History was never so much fun—you won't want to miss a single moment!